Michael Moorcock is astonishing. His enormous output includes around fifty novels, innumerable short stories and a rock album. Born in London in 1939, he became editor of *Tarzan Adventures* at sixteen, moving on later to edit the *Sexton Blake Library*. He has earned his living as a writer/editor ever since, and is without doubt one of Britain's most popular and most prolific authors. He has been compared with Tennyson, Tolkein, Raymond Chandler, Wyndham Lewis, Ronald Firbank, Mervyn Peake, Edgar Allan Poe, Colin Wilson, Anatole France, William Burroughs, Edgar Rice Burroughs, Charles Dickens, James Joyce, Vladimir Nabokov, Jorge Luis Borges, Joyce Cary, Ray Bradbury, H.G. Wells, George Bernard Shaw and Hieronymus Bosch, among others.

'No one at the moment in England is doing more to break down the artificial divisions that have grown up in novel writing—realism, surrealism, science fiction, historical fiction, social satire, the poetic novel—than Michael Moorcock'
Angus Wilson

'He is an ingenious and energetic experimenter, restlessly original, brimming over with clever ideas'
Robert Nye, *The Guardian*

Michael Moorcock

My Experiences in the
Third World War

Illustrated by
Jill Riches, R Glyn Joes, Mal Dean, Derek Twiss

SAVOY BOOKS

In association with
NEW ENGLISH LIBRARY
TIMES MIRROR

A Savoy Original Paperback
Savoy Books Ltd 1980

Cover artwork: Michael Heslop

Published by Savoy Books Ltd,
279 Deansgate, Manchester M3 4EW,
ENGLAND

ISBN 0 86130 037 8

For Harlan Ellison, who offered me his cave.

Contents

Introduction

THE THIRD WORLD WAR might not be fought (as one character in this book suggests of the Fourth) in the country of the soul, but it has certainly been fought thousands of times over in the country of fiction. I am amongst that group of writers primarily associated with NEW WORLDS which looked to science fiction for its metaphors, its images, rather than its prospective rationalisations. In that sense we probably produced a kind of 'anti-sf', for we did not rationalise our anxieties, but tried to bring them into the light and examine them, perhaps in the faint hope that examination and analysis might give us some clue as to how we might, for instance, stop WWIII. I currently hold the belief that any large scale future war will be averted (if it is averted) simply from fear, from the knowledge of the irreversible consequences of engaging in such a war. It is a hard belief for a humanist like myself to come to.

The narrator in the following stories is not me. Indeed, I hope the reader will detect at least one other interpretation of his character, beyond his own way of representing himself. This sort of first person narrative (Henry James refined it, but he had his precursers), attempting to offer clues as to the nature of the narrator and his own areas of self-deception and subjectivity, is fairly hard to do (I recently completed a novel, BYZANTIUM ENDURES, using this technique) but hopes to provide an additional level of understanding. The narrator is revealed not so much by what he says as by what he selects to say to the reader.

One of the reasons for so much experiment in recent years has been the desire to find narrative forms which will, with luck, carry an increased load of subject matter and implication. One loots from the past. 17th, 18th, 19th and 20th century developments in the art of fiction all have to be studied and, if useful, employed. One is never doing anything entirely fresh; any freshness, I suppose, comes from what an individual writer can supply. *My Experiences in the Third World War* are examples of current experiments of mine. *The Dodgem Division*, a hitherto unreprinted Jerry Cornelius story (originally published in SPECULATION), is an example of one of my first experiments (it now seems pretty primitive). *Peace On Earth* was the first adult sf story I published (Barry Bayley expanded it because Ted Carnell of NEW WORLDS thought it too short) and *The Love Beast* is included here because it has not been reprinted for years (I suppose for good reason) and I have, through the offices of Savoy Books, the opportunity to indulge myself by putting a good deal of my juvenile work into print. I'm still sufficiently idealistic, moreover, to hope that the message of *The Love Beast* finds an echo in the far more ambitious *Leaving Pasadena*. One of my favourite stories refers to the exodus of Hungarians into the film industry before the Second World War. On a certain motion picture lot someone, out of frustration, put up a sign: *To be Hungarian is not enough. One must also work.* To say it another way: You can't just talk the talk, you must also walk the walk. So much for my own spot of moralising.

Naturally, I continue to hope that this book will be published before the outbreak of the Third World War.

Michael Moorcock
Ladbroke Grove
March 1980

Michael Moorcock

One

Going to Canada

I WAS ORDERED to Canada; that pie-dish of privilege and broken promises: to Toronto. My chief was uncomprehending when I showed disappointment. "Canada! Everybody wants to go there."

"I have stayed in Toronto before," I told him.

He knew. He became suspicious, so I said that I had been joking. I chuckled to confirm this. His old, Great Russian face, moulded by the imposition of a dozen conflicting tyrannies, made a little mad smile. "You are to look up Belko, an emigré. He is the only Belko in the phone book."

"Very well, Victor Andreyevitch." I accepted the colourful paper wallet of tickets and money. This supply was an unusual one. My 'front' normally allowed me to be self-supporting. I work as an antique-dealer in the Portobello Road.

"Belko knows why you are meeting him. He will tell you what you have to know. It concerns some American planes, I gather."

I shook hands and descended the green-carpeted stairs into the rain of East London.

DURING OUR CIVIL War many pretended to be Bolsheviks in order to terrorise local communities. After the war these people had continued as commissars. It had been their class which had gradually ousted most of the original Marxists. Stalin became their leader and examplar. My father had been a member of that embryonic aristocracy.

Like the order it had replaced, our aristocracy had been founded on banditry and maintained by orthodox piety. I was a younger son without much of a patrimony. Previously I might have gone into the priesthood or the army. I went into the modern combination of both, the KGB. The KGB is a far more conventional and congenial profession than most Westerners imagine. There I enjoyed myself first as a minor bureaucrat in a Moscow department, later as a special officer on one of our passenger ships plying between Leningrad and New York, Odessa and Sydney. Later still I became a plant in London where until recently I lived for twelve relatively uneventful years. I flattered myself that my background and character suited me to the role of a seedy near-alcoholic dealer in old furniture and over-priced bric-a-brac. It was believed that I was a Polish expatriate and indeed I had taken the name and British passport of just such an emigré; he had returned voluntarily to Poland on a whim and had sold his old identity to us in a perfectly amiable arrangement. We eased his way with the Cracow authorities who granted him new papers and found him a flat and a job.

My name in London was Tomas Dobrowsky. For my own amusement I preferred the name of Tom Conrad. It was this name, in thirties 'modern' lettering, which adorned my shop. I paid taxes, VAT, and owned a TV licence. Although I had no particular desire to maintain my part forever, I enjoyed it for its complete lack of anxiety and the corresponding sense of security it gave me. Now that I was to return briefly to the real world, I should have to seek a fresh *context*.

A Soviet citizen requires a *context*, because his conditioning makes him a permanent child. Anything will do. Therefore the *context* is often simple slavery. Even I, of Jewish Ukrainian extraction (through my grandmother), need that sense of boundaries. It is probably no coincidence that Kropotkin, founder of modern anarchism, was a Russian: his defiant views are directly opposed to our needs, which are on the whole of an authoritarian nature.

My father had been a naval petty officer. Later he became 'commissar' of a small town in Belorussia. He had eleven other deserting sailors with him when he had arrived in early 1918. They represented themselves as Bolsheviks. He had worn a leather jacket with two Mauser pistols in his belt and he had rarely taken off his sailor's peaked cap. Somehow the Civil War did not touch the town much, so the gang made the most of its time.

My father took five young girls from the local gymnasium for himself and gave the rest to his men. He instructed the girls in every debauchery. When the Civil War ended and it became obvious who had won, my father did not do away with the girls (as he might well have—it was common practice) but made them read to him from the works of Marx and Engels, from Lenin's writings, from *Pravda* and *Izhvestia*, until he and they were all familiar with the new dogma. Then he formed his thugs into the nucleus of the local Party, sent four of the girls (now fully-fledged Komsomol leaders) back to the gymnasium as teachers, and married Vera Vladimirovna, my mother.

In time he was praised for his example to the community and was awarded a medal by the State. During the famines of the next few years he and my mother were never hungry. During the purges they never seemed to be in danger. They had two children, a boy and a girl.

In 1936 my father went off on Party business and in 1938 I was born. The young writer who begat me was subsequently sent to a camp and died. I had long considered myself the secret guardian of his blood. My father was in most respects a realist. He preferred to accept me as his own rather than risk the scandal of his name being associated with that of the writer. My older sister was killed in the War. My older brother became a hero during the Siege of Stalingrad. He ran a large power-plant near Smolensk on the Dnieper. He was a self-satisfied, right-thinking man.

"A little pain," my mother used to say to her friends, "makes good girls of us all."

My father trained his girls to kiss his feet, his legs, his private parts, his arse. My mother was more wholehearted at this than her rivals, which is how he came to pick her as his wife. Again, she behaved in a Russian way. She was dutiful in all things, but, when his authority was absent, she became irresponsible. The Russian soul is a masochist's wounds. It is a frightening, self-indulgent, monumentally sentimental relinquishing of individual responsibility: it is schizophrenic. More than elsewhere, personal suffering is equated with virtue.

My grandmother was apparently raped by a young Jew and my mother was the result. The Jew was killed shortly afterwards, in a general pogrom resulting from the affair. That was in Ekaterinaslav privince in the last years of the nineteenth century. My grandmother never would say for certain that it had been rape. I remember her winking at me when the word was mentioned. I remember meeting my great-uncle, the surviving brother of the dead man. He told me that after the Revolution some Red Cossacks came to his shtetl. He was mortally afraid, of course, and would have done anything to stay alive. A Cossack named Konkoff billeted himself in my great-uncle's house. My great-uncle was mindless with terror, grovelling before the Cossack, ready to lick the soles off his boots at the first demand. Instead, Konkoff had laughed at him, offered him some rations, pulled him upright, patted him on the back and called him 'comrade'. My great-uncle realised that the revolution had actually changed things. He was no longer a detested animal. He had become a Cossack's pet Jew.

In Russia, in those days before the present War, there had been a resurgence of Nationalism, encouraged by the State. Because of the absence of real democratic power, many had turned (as they did under Tsarism) to Pan-Slavism. A direct consequence of this movement was anti-Semitism, also blessed unofficially by the State, and a spirit amongst our élite which, while not so unequivocally anti-Semitic, was reminiscent of the Black Hundreds or the Legion of the Archangel Michael, the early 20th century pogromists. It was obvious that the State equated radicalism with intellectual Jewish trouble-makers. The State therefore encouraged—through the simple prejudices of its cunning but not considerably intelligent leaders—a movement in no way dissimilar to that which had followed the troubles of 1905, when Jewish socialists had been scapegoats for everything. Stalin had eliminated virtually the entire Jewish element of the Party, of course, by 1935.

When I was young it had been fashionable to scoff at the trappings of Nationalism—at folk costumes, at peasant blouses and so on. Outside of cultural exhibitions and performances these things were a sign of old-fashioned romanticism. They were not considered progressive. When I returned to

Russia briefly in 1980 young people were walking the streets looking as if they had stepped out of a performance of *Prince Igor*. Even some of the younger leaders would on occasions be photographed in Cossack costume. Anti-semitic books and paintings, even songs, received official patronage. The authoritarian republic had at last, in sixty years, managed to resemble in detail the autocracy it had replaced. Soon there would be no clear differences save that poverty and sickness had been abolished in the Slavic regions of the Union.

These benefits had been gained by relinquishing dignity and liberty, and the nobler forms of idealism which had given the early Revolution its rhetoric and its impetus. There were no longer any private arts. Everything had been sacrificed to formalised ceremonies similar to Church ritual or other primitive affirmations of superstition. The Soviet Union had codified and sanctified this terrifying impulse of human beings to shout reassuring lies to one another while standing with eyes tight shut on the brink of a chasm of reality. The State pretended that it was impossible (or at very least immoral) for such a chasm to exist. Soviet bureaucracy, too, formalised human failing and gave it shape and respectability: it did not merely accept this failing: it exalted it. I was as conditioned as anyone to believe that our lobotomising methods of ordering the human condition were the most sensible. I found all these aspects of Soviet life comforting and reassuring. I had no wish to emigrate. I did not have the character necessary for the enjoyment of personal freedom. Moreover, I could not bear to face an old age in which the Russian language was denied me.

In spite of appalling distortions and neulogisms, there remains no more beautiful and subtle a language in the world than Russian; none more musical; none more representative of the soul of the people who speak it. Its roots are in Old Slavonic, in Church Slavonic; in blood and dark ignorance of a nature almost impossible for an Anglo-Saxon or a Latin to understand: We have in this respect more in common with the Celts. We have no ethical system as such, merely a philosophy of life based firmly on the dignity of pain, on fear of the unknown, and suspicion of anything we cannot at once recognise. That is why Bolshevism was so attractive an ideology to many peasants who identified it with a benevolently modified Church and Monarchy and for a time believed that Lenin intended to restore the Tsar to his throne; it is why it was so quickly adapted to Russian needs and Russian methods. I do not disapprove of the government of the Soviet Union. I accept it as a necessity. In 1930, as a result of the bourgeois Revolution headed by Kerenski, and the Revolution initiated by the bourgeois Lenin, women and children were starving to death all over Russia. Stalin was at heart an Orthodox peasant. He and other Orthodox peasants saved Russia from the monster released upon the nation by foolish, middle-class idealists. In doing so he punished the Communists who had brought about the disaster: the intellectuals and fanatics who were truly to blame for our misfortunes.

Stalin took on the great burden and responsibilities of a Tsar and all his ministers. Stalin knew that History would revile him and that his followers would become cynical and cruel. He countered their cynicism and cruelty with the only weapon he was able to use: terror. He became mad. He was himself not a cynic. He made factories efficient. He gave us our industry, our education, our health service. He made homes clean and sanitary. He killed millions for the sake of all those other millions who would otherwise have perished. He made it possible for us to round, eventually, on Hitler and drive him back to Germany. He returned to us the security of our Empire. And when he died we destroyed his memory. He knew that we would and I believe that he understood that this would have to happen. He was a realist; but he possessed an Orthodox conscience and his conscience made him mad. I am a realist happily born of an age which countered and adapted Christianity and that is doubtless what makes me such a good and reliable employee of the State.

BECAUSE OF THE increasingly strict controls applied to those who wished to travel to and from Canada, it was necessary for me to go to my doctor for a medical certificate. I used a fashionable private doctor in South Kensington who was quick to prescribe the drugs I required. In his waiting-room I found three young women wearing the elaborate and violent make-up and costume then favoured by the British demi-monde. They were whispering together in a peculiar way common only to whores and nuns, full of sudden shifts of volume and tone and oblique reference, glances and gestures, so I only heard snatches of their conversation.

"I was doing this job, you know—straight... At the club. He said he wanted me to work for him—you know—so I said I wouldn't—he said to go out with him—but I wouldn't—he was a funny guy, you know—he gave me this—" A bandaged arm was held up. It was a soft arm in a soft dress. "He had a bottle, you know—they called the cops—they're prosecuting—his lawyer phoned me and offered me thirty thousand to settle out of court..."

"Settle," advised one of the other girls.

"I would," said the second.

"But my lawyer says we can get fifty."

"Settle for thirty."

"He gave me seventeen stitches." All this was relayed in a neutral, almost self-satisfied tone. "What you doing here, anyway?"

"I just came with her," said the prettiest. "It's about her pills."

"I came to get my slimming pills changed. Those others make me feel really sick, you know."

"What! Duothons?"

"Yeah. They make me feel terrible."

"What you going to ask him for? Terranin?"

"They're what I use," said her friend.

"They're much better," agreed the wounded whore. "You're looking different," she told the girl's friend. "I wouldn't have recognised you. You're looking terrible."

They all laughed.

"Did you know what happened to Mary?" She put her mouth close to the girl's ear and began to whisper rapidly.

The doctor's receptionist opened the door. "You can go in now, Miss Williams."

"...all over the bed," finished Miss Williams, rising and following the receptionist.

When she had gone the other two began to discuss her in a disinterested fashion, as if they followed some unconscious habit. Neither, it emerged, believed that thirty thousand pounds had been offered. "More like three," said one. They, too, were not at all outraged by the event. Most whores are frightened of any demonstration of passion, which is why they choose masters who treat them coldly. I had for a short while been in charge of a whore-house in Greece and had learned how to deal with the girls who were conditioned to confuse love with fear. If they were afraid of their master they thought they loved him. Because they were not afraid of their clients they could not love them and in the main felt contempt for them. But it was self-contempt they actually felt. I remembered with some dismay the single-mindedness of such girls who pursued persecution and exploitation as an anodyne, as their customers often pursued sexual sensation; who learned to purchase the favours of their employers with the very money they received from the hire of their own bodies. My spell as a whore-master had been the only time I had tasted direct power and it had taken every ounce of self-discipline to administer; it was a relief to become what I now was.

Miss Williams rejoined her friends. "I'm going to have it photographed this afternoon," she told them, pulling down her sleeve.

The two girls went in to the doctor. They came out. All three left together.

I was next in the surgery. The doctor smiled at me. "More trouble?"

I shook my head.

"The penicillin worked?"

"Yes."

"It's funny that. Acts like a shot on syphilis, won't touch gonorrhoea. Well, what's the trouble?" He spoke rapidly in a high-pitched voice. He was a Jew.

"None. I just need a certificate to say I'm not suffering from anything a Canadian's likely to catch."

He laughed. "That depends on you, doesn't it?" He was already reaching for his pad of forms. "Canada, eh? Lucky you."

He filled in the form swiftly and handed it to me. "Going for long?"

"I don't think so," I said.

"Business?"

"Believe it or not, we're buying our antiques from North America these days." It was true.

"No! Really?" He was amused. He stood up as I stood up. He leaned across his desk to shake hands. "Well, good luck. Enjoy yourself."

"I will."

I left his surgery and began to walk up Kensington Church Street, passing the three girls who were waiting on the kerb for a taxi. One of them looked very much like the girl who had given me syphilis. I wondered if she would recognise me as I went by. But she was too deep in conversation to notice, even though I walked to within an inch or two of her shoulder, close enough to identify her heavy perfume.

THE MORNING OF the day I was due to take the overnight plane from Gatwick (it was a budget flight) I read the news of a border clash between China and India, but I did not give it too much attention. The Russo-Indian Pact had been signed the previous year, in Simla, and I believed that the Chinese would take the pact seriously. By the afternoon the radio news reported Moscow's warnings to Peking. When I left for Gatwick on the train from Victoria, I bought an evening paper. I had begun to consider the possibility of war between Russia and China. The evening news was vague and told me no more than had the radio news. On the plane, which took off on schedule, I watched a Walt Disney film about two teenage girls who seemed to be twins.

I reached Toronto at eleven o'clock in the evening, local time, took a taxi to a downtown hotel and turned on the television to discover that Soviet troops and tanks were invading China while Indian forces, with some British and American divisions already stationed there, were moving towards the Chinese border. A newsflash brought the information that both the Warsaw Pact countries and the NATO countries had lent their support to India and that China and her allies were expected to capitulate very soon.

Early the next day I found myself in a pleasant suburban street of tall, Victorian wooden houses, birch-trees and maples and soft lawns, ringing the bell of my contact, Mr Belko. An angry girl, a pudgy seventeen, came to the door. She was wearing a blue dressing gown.

"Mr Belko is expecting me," I told her.

She was triumphant. "Mr Belko left an hour ago."

"Where did he go? Would you mind?"

"To the airport. Hadn't you heard? It's World War Three!"

For a moment I was amused by the inevitability of her

remark; the assumption, moreover, of the inevitable event.

"You look beat," she said. "Are you a diplomat?"

"Not really."

She grew to feeling guilty. "Come in and have some coffee."

"I accept. Thank you."

Her mother was at breakfast in the large, modern kitchen. "Dubrowski," I said, removing my hat. "I am so sorry..."

"Vassily's left. Janet told you?"

"Yes." I unbuttoned my overcoat. Janet took it. I thanked her. I sat down at the table. I was brought a cup of that Western coffee which smells so good but does not taste of anything. I drank it.

"Was it important?" asked Janet's mother.

"Well..."

"To do with the crisis?"

I was not sure. I waved a palm.

"Well," said Janet's mother, "you're lucky to be here, that's all I can say."

"You think there will be a full-scale war?" I accepted sugar from the young girl's hands.

"Let them fight it out," said Janet's mother. "Get it over with."

"It will involve Canada."

Janet's mother buttered some toast. "Not directly."

"Are you Ukrainian, too?" said Janet.

"Too?"

"We're Ukrainians." Janet sat down beside me. I became aware of her warmth. "Or at least momma and poppa are."

I looked at the woman in the housecoat with her dyed red hair, her make-up, her American way of slouching against the table. I wondered if I were not enduring some kind of complicated test.

"I came over in 1947," said Janet's mother. "From England. We'd been deported during the German occupation and when the allies arrived we managed to get to England. Fedya was born here. Are you Ukrainian?"

I began to laugh a little. It was a feeble titter, but it was the first spontaneous expression of emotion I had had in years. "Yes," I said. "I am."

"We haven't really stayed in touch much," said Janet's

mother, "with the Community here, you know. Janet's been to some meetings. She sees more of the old people than we do. She's a Nationalist, aren't you, dear?"

"Convinced," said Janet.

"Canadian," I asked, "or Ukrainian?" I was genuinely confused.

Janet took this well. She put youthful fingers on my sleeve. "Both," she said.

When I returned to my hotel I found a note telling me to go to our embassy. At the embassy I was ordered to fly direct to Moscow on the next Aeroflot flight. There I would be briefed about my new role. By the time I reached Moscow, Allied troops were already withdrawing from China and an agreement was being negotiated in the United Nations. I was given a Soviet passport and told to return to London.

My brief stay in Moscow had made me homesick. I would have been grateful for a holiday in the country for a week or two. I have yet to have my dream fulfilled. A month after I got back, the real War broke and I, in common with so many others, began to taste the euphoria of Armageddon.

(London, November 1978,
Los Angeles, November 1979)

Leaving Pasadena

I WAS ASKED by the woman why I had no pity. She sat on the floor, her elbow resting upon a couch, her head in her hand. She had not wept. Her anguish had tempered her eyes: they glittered with unvoiced needs. I could not touch her. I could not insult her with my compassion. I told her that pity was an inappropriate emotion. Our world was burning and there was no time for anything but rapid action. Africa and Australia were already gone. The clouds and the contamination were a matter of anxiety to those who survived. She told me, in slow, over-controlled syllables, that she was probably dying. She needed love, she said. I told her she should find someone, therefore, whose needs matched her own. My first loyalty was to my unit. I could not reach my hand to her. Any gesture would have been cruel.

The other two women came into the room. One had my bag. "You still don't know where you're going?" said the blonde, Julia. Her fashionably garish cosmetics appeared to give her face the lustre and texture of porcelain.

I turned my back and walked into the hallway. "Not yet."

Julia said: "I'll try to look after her."

As I got to the front door of the apartment, the brown-haired women, Honour, said: "You pious bastard." She wore no make-up. Her face was as pale as Julia's.

I accepted her accusation. I had at that moment nothing left but piety and I would not dignify it with words. I nodded, shook hands with them both. I heard her mumbling some despairing question from the room, then I had walked down the white steps of the Pasadena condominium, crossed the courtyard with its silenced fountain, its poised cherubs, brilliant in the sun, and entered the car which had been sent to collect me. I was leaving California. That was all I had been told.

My chief had a rented house in Long Beach, near the marina. We drove to it through avenues of gigantic palms until we reached the almost deserted freeway. Vehicles kept well apart, considering the others warily. Only government people had official driving permits; anyone else could be psychotic or a criminal.

Long Beach was still populated. There were even people sailing their yachts into the harbour. The Pacific threat seemed to bother the people only as much as they had been bothered by the threat of earthquakes. The houses were low and calm, divided by shrubs and trees, with neat grass. I saw a man riding a pony across his lawn. He waved sardonically at the car. Groups of women stared at the limousine with expressions of contempt. We found my chief's house. The chauffeur went to tell him we were there. He came out immediately.

As he stopped to join me, the chief said: "You look bad. You should sleep more."

I told him, dutifully, about the woman. He was sympathetic. "There's a war on. It's how it is in War." Naturally, I agreed with him. "We are fighting for their good, after all," he added.

We drove to a military airfield. Both Soviet and U.S. planes were there. We went immediately to our Ilyushin, and had scarcely settled in the uncomfortable seats before we took off.

My chief handed me a passport. It had my real name and a recent photograph. "You're officially with the liason staff, at last," he said. "It means you can report either to the Americans or to us. Nothing will be kept back. Matters are too urgent now." I expressed appropriate surprise.

I looked down on Los Angeles; its beaches, its fantasies. It was like setting aside a favourite story as a child. We headed inland over mountains, going East.

"The Third World War has already been fought," said my chief, "in the third world, as the Americans call it. Why else would they call it that? This is actually the Fifth World War."

"What was the Fourth?" I asked.

"It was fought in the country of the soul."

I laughed. I had forgotten his sentimentality. "Who won?"

"Nobody. It merely prepared us for this."

There were clouds beneath us. It seemed to become calm as the altitude encouraged deafness. I could hardly hear his next remark: "It has sharpened our wits and deadened our emotional responses. War is a great relief, eh? A completely false sense of objectivity. The strain to remain grown-up is too much for most of us."

It was familiar stuff from him. I unfastened my seat-belt and walked clumsily along the plane to where a Cossack sergeant served at a small bar. I ordered some of the Finnish vodka we had recently acquired. I drank the glass down and returned to my place. Four high-ranking officers in tropical uniforms were arguing in the seats behind me. One of them was of the opinion that we should begin full-scale rocket attacks on major Chinese cities. The others were for caution. The bombing had, after all, been stopped. Most of the civilised countries were still unharmed.

My chief began coughing. It was that dry noise usually associated with smoke inhalation. He recovered himself and in answer to my concerned expression told me that he was probably getting a cold. "We should be in Washington soon. All this travelling about is bad for the constitution." He shrugged. "But life is never easy. Even in wartime."

An official car met us at the airport. It bore the arms of the President. We passed the monstrous neo-classical buildings which celebrated that naive 18th century rationalism we all now regretted and from which we seemed to be suffering at present. We arrived at a modern block of government offices. In the elevator my chief told me not to show surprise at whatever we discussed. He believed that we were thought to know more than we had actually been told.

A bland, smooth-faced man in a light-coloured suit introduced himself as Mansfield and offered us deep, black chairs. He asked us about our journey, about California, and told us of the people living along the West Coast. "People learn to identify their homes with their security. When something like this happens... Well, we all know about the Jews refusing to leave Germany."

"Your newspapers contradict themselves," said my chief. He smiled. "They say there is little to fear."

"True." Mansfield offered us Lucky Strike cigarettes which we accepted. My chief coughed a little before he took a light.

"We think you'll have more success in Venezuela." Mansfield returned the lighter to his desk. "They are suspicious of our motives, naturally."

"And not of ours?" My chief continued to smile.

"They could believe your arguments better. They are not too sure if the alliance will maintain itself. You might be able to persuade them."

"Possibly."

"They can't stay neutral much longer."

"Why not?"

"Because someone will attack them."

"Then perhaps we should wait until that happens. It would be easier to liberate them, eh?"

"We need their oil. This freeze of theirs is pointless. It does nobody any good."

"And why do you want us to go?"

"The Russians?"

"No." My chief waved a hand at me. "Us."

"We have to contact their intelligence first. After that the politicians can sort things out."

"You've made arrangements?"

"Yes. It was thought best not to meet in Caracas. You'll go to Maracaibo. It's where the oil is, anyway. Most of their oil» people want to sell. We're not certain of the attitudes you'll find, but we understand that there is a lot of pressure from that side."

"You have material for us?"

Mansfield lifted a folder from his desk and showed it to us.

Although my chief seemed to be taking the meeting seriously, I began to wonder at the vagueness of its content. I suspected that our going to Maracaibo would have no affect at all. We were going because it was something to do.

I resisted an urge, when we reached our hotel in Maracaibo, to telephone the woman and ask how she was. It would do her no good, I decided, for her to hear from me. I knew that, in other circumstances, I would have loved her. She had done me several favours in the course of my work, so I was also grateful to her. The sense of gratitude was the only indulgence I allowed myself.

My chief walked through the connecting door into my room. He rubbed his eyebrows. "I have a meeting with a member of their intelligence. A colonel. But it is to be a one to one thing. You're free to do what you like this evening. I have the name of a house."

"Thank you." I wrote down the address he gave me.

"It will do you good," he said. He was sympathetic. "And one of us might as well enjoy the pleasures of the town. I hear the whores are of a high quality."

"I am much obliged to you." I would go, I thought, only because I had no wish to stay in my room the whole time. His giving me leave confirmed my suspicion that there was no real reason for us being in Maracaibo.

The town, with its skyscrapers and remnants of Spanish-style architecture, was well-lit and relatively clean. I had once been told that 'Venezuela is the future'. They had been experimenting with different energy sources, using their oil income to develop systems which would not be much dependant on oil. But Maracaibo seemed very little different, save that the lake itself, full of machinery and rigging, occasionally gave off mysterious puffs of flame which would illuminate buildings and create uncertain shadows. There was a stink of oil about the place. As I walked, local map in hand, to the address my chief had given me I saw one of their airships, built by a British firm at Cardington, sail into the darkness beyond the city. Venezuela had been perhaps the last country to associate romance with practical engineering.

I reached the house. It was large and fairly luxurious. The decor was comfortable and lush in the manner of some of the more grandiose family restaurants I had visited in Pasadena. There was a pianist playing similar music to his American counterpart. There was a bar. I sat down and ordered a Scotch. I was approached by a pretty hostess who wore a blonde wig. Her skin was dark and her smile was wide and seemed genuine. In English she said that she thought she had seen me there before. I told her that this was only my second visit to Maracaibo. She asked if I were Swedish. I said that I was Russian. She kissed me and said that she loved Russian people, that they knew how to enjoy themselves. "Lots of vodka," she said. But I was drinking Scotch; was I an emigre? I said, from habit, that I was. Her name was Anna. Her father, she said, had been born in South London. Did I know London? Very well, I said. I had lived there for some years. Anna wondered if Brixton were like Maracaibo. I said there were some similarities. We look for familiarity in the most unlikely circumstances before we accept what is strange to us. It is as true of travellers as it is of lovers.

Anna brought a girl for me. She had fine black hair tied back from her face; a white dress with a great deal of lace. She looked about sixteen. Her make-up was subtle. She pretended to be shy. I found her appealing. Her name was Maria, she told me. She spoke excellent English with an American accent. I bought her a drink, expecting to go to her room, but she said she would like to take me home, if that suited me. I decided against caution. She led me outside and we drove in a taxi to a street of what seemed to be quiet, middle-class apartment buildings. We climbed two flights of stairs. She opened a well-polished wooden door with her key and we entered an apartment full of quality furniture in subdued good taste. I began to suspect I had been picked up by a schoolgirl and that this was her parents' home. But the way she moved in it, getting me another Scotch, switching on the overhead fan, taking my jacket, convinced me that she was the mistress of the place. Moreover, I knew that she was actually older than sixteen; that she cultivated the appearance of a teenager. I began to experience a reluctance to go to bed with her. Against my will I remembered the woman in Pasadena. I forced myself towards that belief that all women were, after all, the same, that it satisfied them to give themselves up to a man. The whore, at least, would make money from her instincts. The woman in Pasadena came by nothing but pain. We went into the bedroom and undressed. In the large and comfortable white bed I eventually confessed that I was in no haste to make love to her. I had been unable to adjust my mood. I asked her why she had shaved her pubic hair. She said that it increased her own pleasure and besides many men found it irrestible. She began to tell me her story. She had been, she said, in love with the man who introduced her to prostitution. Evidently she was still obsessed by him, because it required no great expression of interest from me for her to tell me the whole story. It was familiar enough. What she said, of course, was couched in the usual sort of sentimentality and romanticism. She mentioned love a great deal and her knowledge that, although he did not say so, he really loved her and cared for her and it was only right, because she loved him, that he should be allowed to be the way he was. He had many other girls, of course, including, I gathered, a wife. Initially Maria had, in the manner of despairing women, attempted to make of herself an improved piece of capital: she had dyed her hair, shaved her pubis, painted her face and nails. The girl-whore is always highly valued wherever one goes in the world. I gathered that while the man had appreciated the gesture he had told her that he intended to continue seeing other women. All this was depressing, for I was never particularly interested in economics. I found myself moralising a trifle. I told her that maturity and self-possession were in the end more attractive qualities to me. They guaranteed me a certain kind of freedom based on mutually accepted responsibility. She did not understand a word, of course. I added that a woman's attempts to use a man as her context were thoroughly understood by someone like myself. I had my loyalties. But, like most men, I was not able to be either a woman's nation or her cause. Maria made some attempt to rouse me and then fell back. She said that it was her bad luck to pick up a bore. She had thought I would be interesting. She added that she did not feel she could charge me much. I was amused. I got up and telephoned the hotel. The chief had not yet returned. I said that I would stay longer, in that case. She said that she would enjoy my company, but I would have to be more entertaining. Eventually I achieved a reasonable state of mind and made love to her. She was soft, yielding and foul-mouthed. She was able to bring me to a more than satisfactory orgasm. As I left, she insisted that I telephoned her the next day if I could. I agreed that I would if it were at all possible.

My chief was jovial when we breakfasted together in his room. "We have at least a week here," he said. "There are subtleties. These people are worse than the Arabs."

I reported the girl. He shrugged. "You have nothing to reveal. Even if it is some kind of strategy, they would be wasting their time."

I had the impression that he had brought me here on holiday. In the outside world, the news was not good. A bomb had landed somewhere in India and no-one was absolutely certain where it had come from. No major city had been hit. This was not acceptable warfare, said my chief. War was supposed to cut down on ambiguities.

I telephoned the girl from the breakfast table. I arranged to see her for lunch.

We ate in a smart restaurant at the top of a modern tower. There was mist on the lake and Maracaibo was covered in pale gold light. She wore a red suit with a matching hat. She was gentle and obviously amused by what she saw as my stiffness. She had a way of making me relax. Naturally, I resisted falling too much under her spell.

After lunch, she took us to a quay. Several men in tattered nautical clothes called to her. She spoke to one of them and then we had climbed down into a small, elegant motorboat. She started the engine, took the wheel, and we rode out into the mist.

I asked her what her man thought of all this. She became gay. "He doesn't care."

"But you are making no money."

"It's not really like that," she said. "He's kind, you know. Or can be."

The whole episode had the character of a lull in a singularly bad storm. I could not entirely rid my mind of the knowledge of the woman in Pasadena, but I could think of no better way of spending my time. Maria steered the boat inexpertly past a series of oil derricks which stood in the water like stranded and decapitated giraffes. A breeze began to part the mist. I had the impression of distant mountains.

She stopped the engine and we embraced. She suggested that we fuck. "It's always been an ambition of mine," she said.

I did my best, but the boat was uncomfortable and my body was too tired. I eventually brought her to orgasm with my mouth. She seemed more than contented. After a while she got up and returned to the wheel. "You look happier," she said. "So do you," I replied. I was hard put not to feel affection for her. But that sense of affection did me no good because it recalled the woman in Pasadena. I began to tell her a joke about the War. Some Chinese commandos had entered what they thought was Indian territory and completely destroyed one of their own bases. She became serious. "Will the War reach Venezuela?"

"Almost certainly," I said. "Unless a few people come to their senses. But there has been no true catharsis yet."

She asked me what I meant. I said: "No orgasm, eh?"

"My God," she said.

On the quay, we agreed to meet at the same spot that evening. "I want to show you the lake at night." She looked up suddenly and pointed. There was a soft sound of engines. It was another airship, white and painted with the Venezuelan military colours. Reassessed technology was to have been the salvation of the world. Now this country would be lucky if it escaped complete destruction. I said nothing of this to Maria.

When I was first ordered to work abroad I felt I was going into exile. The territory was unfamiliar, offering dangers I could not anticipate. I saw Maria to her taxi and walked back to my hotel. For some reason I was reminded, perhaps by a sign or a face on the street, of the strange suburb-ghetto of Watts, where everyone lived better than almost anyone in the Soviet Union. It had amused me to go there. They had food stamps: the young have never known a breadline. One had hoped to match America. Before the War, we were only a short distance behind on the road to discontented capitalism. Beyond that was anarchy, which cannot appeal to me, although I know it was supposed to have been our goal.

I bought a Polish-language newspaper. It was over a week old and I could barely understand the references. The newspaper was published in New York. But I enjoyed the feel of the print. I read it as I lay in my bath. My chief telephoned. He sounded drunk. It occurred to me that he, too, believed himself to be on vacation. He told me that I was free for the evening.

Maria had two friends with her when I arrived at the quay. They were both some years older than she and wore the sort of heavy 'forties make-up which had been fashionable a few years previously in the West. Their cotton dresses, one pink and one yellow, followed the same style, as did their hair. They wore very strong perfume and looked like versions of Rita Hayworth. They were far more self-conscious than Maria. She said they spoke little English and apologised for bringing them along. Her explanation was vague, consisting mainly of shrugs and raised brows. I made no objection. I was content to enjoy the close presence of so much femininity.

Once again, Maria drove us out into the twilight. The water seemed to brighten as it became blacker. The two older women sat together behind Maria and myself. They produced some Mexican Tequila and passed the bottle. Soon we were all fairly drunk. When Maria stopped the boat in the middle of the lake again, we all rolled together in one another's arms. I realised that this was part of Maria's plan. Another fantasy she wished to experience. I allowed the women to have their way with me, although I was not of much use to them. It gave me considerable pleasure to watch them making love. Maria took no part in this, but observed and directed, giggling the whole time. The unreality was disarming. The situation was no stranger than the situation in the world at large. It seemed that I moved from one dream to another and that this dream, given the cheerfulness of everyone involved, was preferable to the rest. I knew now that Maria felt safe with me, because I controlled my emotions so thoroughly and because I was a stranger. I knew that I was proving of help to her and this made me happy. I thought of warning her that in seeking catharsis through her sexuality she could lose touch with the source of her feelings, lose her lovers, lose her bearings, but it did not seem to matter. With the War threatening to become more widespread our futures were all so thoroughly in doubt that we might as well enjoy what we could of the present.

Several days and nights passed. Each time we met, Maria would propose another sexual escapade and I would agree. My own curiosity was satisfied, as was my impulse to believe myself of use to someone. My chief continued to be drunk and wave me on, even when I reported exactly what was happening. As I grew to know her better I believed that she was desperately anxious to become a woman, to escape the form of security in which she now found herself. Her need for instantaneous maturity, her greedy reaching for experience, however painful, was in itself childish. She had indulged herself and been indulged for so long that her means of achieving liberty were crude and often graceless. And yet liberty, maturity might gradually come to her, earned through trauma and that feminine willingness to find fulfillment in despair. There was no doubt that her activities, her attitudes, disguised a considerable amount of despair and emotional confusion. I wondered if I were not exploiting her, even though superficially she seemed to be exploiting me. We were, I determined, merely making reasonable use of one another's time. And in the meanwhile, I recalled, there was the figure of her protector, Ramirez. He presumably knew what was happening, just as my chief knew. I began to feel a certain fondness for him, a certain gratitude. I told Maria that I should like to meet him. This did not appeal to her, but she said she would let him know what I had said. I told her that I would let her know when I was leaving, so that the meeting, if it occurred, could be on my last night. I also warned her that I might be forced to leave suddenly. She said that she had guessed this. On one level, I realised, I was asking her to give up the only power she had. I made some drunken remarks about people who surround themselves with ambiguity in order to maintain their course. They are eventually trapped by the conditions they have created, become confused and begin to question almost every aspect of their own judgement. I felt a certain amount of self-disgust after this statement. I had no business offering Maria a moral education. But political habits are hard to lose.

Puzzled, she told me that she thought Ramirez meant security for her. Yet she knew that she had no desire to marry him. She would not be happy if, tomorrow, he came to her and offered her his all. We laughed together at this. Women marry for security, I remarked, while men often marry merely for the promise of regular sex. The man is inclined to keep his side of the marriage bargain because it is fairly clear. But the woman, having no idea of what the bargain was, is baffled when the man complains.

"Are all marriages like that?" she asked. She had doubtless

had many customers who had verified this. I said no, not all. I knew of several very satisfactory marriages. By and large, however, in countries where political or religious orthodoxy held sway, sexual relationships became extremely confused. Again I had lost her. I became bored with my own simplifications. As we made love, I found myself desperately yearning for the woman in Pasadena.

Maria began to speak more and more of Ramirez. I was now a confessor. From what she said I formed an opinion of him. He was tight-fisted but had made his caution and lack of generosity into a creed so that it sometimes seemed he was expressing self-discipline and neutrality, whereas he was actually indulging himself absolutely. As a result he had begun to fail in business (her flat was threatened), partly through an inability to risk capital, partly through the loss of nerve which comes when security is equated with material goods and well-being. His was a typical dilemma of the middle-class, but she had no way of knowing that since she had spent most of her life in a working class, or bohemian environment. This materialism extended into his sex-life, as is so frequently the case: he hoped to get something for nothing if he could (his life was a series of deals) but expected a good return on any expenditure. He was attractive, boyish and emotionally somewhat naive. These qualities appealed, needless to say, to many women, not all of them childless. He was easily understood and fairly easy to manipulate. Moreover, the woman had some sense of control over the relationship, for such men can also be, on certain levels, highly impressionable: they are nearly all ego. However, his inability, ultimately, to accept responsibility either for himself or others, made him a frustrating partner and his relationships were inclined to deteriorate after a period in which some reform had been attempted on him and he had become resentful. We are changed only by circumstance, never by will alone. She had, for her part, she said, accepted him gladly for what he was. He was better than most, and more interesting. He was not a fool. Neither am I, I found myself saying. She shook her head. "No. You are a big fool. It is why I'm fond of you." I was astonished.

News came from my chief early that morning that we were due to return to the United States the next day. I saw Maria for lunch and said that I should like to see Ramirez. She made me swear that I was leaving and then arranged to meet later at the quay.

From the quayside we went to a nearby bar. It was an ordinary place, dark and a little seamy. Maria knew many of the regulars, particularly the women, whom she kissed. Ramirez arrived. He wore a good suit of dark blue cloth and I was surprised that he was bearded and had spectacles. He shook hands. His flesh was a little soft and his grasp feminine. He said that he was not sure why he had come, except 'I can resist no request from Maria'. We had several strong drinks. We took the motor boat out into the lake. It was a warm night. He removed his jacket but not his waistcoat and asked me if I sniffed cocaine. I said that I did. As he prepared the drug on a small hand-mirror he informed me that he was Maria's master and allowed her sometimes, as in this case, to play with other men: I should go away now or I might find myself the subject of either blackmail or violence. I was amused when I realised that Maria was deceiving him. I decided to play her game as best I could. I told him that I had run whores in Greece and that I knew he did not possess the character of a true ponce. He was not insulted. We took the cocaine. It was of the best quality. I complimented him. "You understand me, however," he said. I did not reply until we returned to the harbour. When we were out of the boat and standing together, Maria on my right, Ramirez beside the open door of his car, I threatened him with death. I told him that I was an agent of the KGB. He became nervous, made no comment, got into his car and left. Maria, on the way home, was disturbed. she asked me what she was going to do. I told her that she was free to take a number of choices. She said she needed money. I gave her some. We stayed together in her flat through the rest of that night and in the morning drove the boat onto the lake again. When Maracaibo disappeared and we seemed alone in the middle of the still, blue water, she took out a small packet of cocaine and, steadying her thin body against a seat, carefully cut two lines on her compact mirror. I took the first, through an American ten dollar bill. She paused before sniffing half the line into one nostril, half into the other. She smiled at me, weary and intimate. "Well?"

"You'll go back to Ramirez?"

"Not if I can stay at an hotel."

"And if you stay at an hotel?"

"I can earn some money. Could you help me get to America?"

"At present? You're safer here."

"But could you?"

"Only on terms I do not wish to make. I repeat, you're better off here."

"Really?"

"Believe me."

Her dark eyes looked away into the lake. "The future is no better than the past."

I guessed that within a week she would be back with Ramirez; within a year she would be free of him. I started the engine and headed towards the reality of the rigs and refineries. I told Maria that I knew she would survive, if there were any luck in the world at all. She had none of that self-involved sexuality which contains in it a peculiar coldness: the more it is indulged, the more my coldness grows. One meets libertines whose lives are devoted to sex and yet who have gradually lost any sexual generosity. Certain women are the same. They cease to celebrate and come more and more to control. It is the inevitable progress of rationalised romance, as I knew well.

In the hotel my chief notified me suddenly that he was dying. He wanted me, eventually, to go to Kiev as liason officer with a Cossack regiment. "I think it's the best I can offer you," he said. He added that his will-power had failed him. I asked him if he were suffering from radiation poisoning. He said that he was. He would be returning to Long Beach for a short while, but I could stay in Washington if I wished. I would be allowed some leave. I could not begin to guess at the manipulation and persuasion he had exerted in order to gain us both so much time, but I was grateful to him and indicated as much. I had decided, I said, to return to Pasadena.

"Good," he said. "We can take the same plane."

I decided not to telephone ahead but went directly from Burbank airport to Pasadena. Los Angeles was quieter than ever, though there was now some evidence of desertion and vandalism. Most of the cars on the freeways were police vehicles. As I drove my rented Toyota towards the richer suburbs I was stopped twice and had my papers checked:

Now, in the current situation, it had become an advantage in America to possess a Soviet passport and KGB identification.

I drove off the freeway onto South Orange. The wide, palm-shaded streets seemed without texture or density after Maracaibo. A thin dream. Pasadena was a geometrical kindergarten vision of security. Only downtown, amongst the bricks and stones of the original settlement, and at the railroad station, was there a sense of complexity at all, and that was the complexity of any small American rural town. I yearned for Europe, for London and its mysterious, claustrophobic streets.

I parked in the communal garages, took my bag from the back seat and walked along the neat crazy-paving to the end block of the condominium. Like so much Los Angeles building it was less than ten years old and beginning to show signs of decay beneath the glaring white glaze. I walked up the steps, glad of the shade, and rang the bell on the right of the double doors. I stopped and picked up a folded newspaper, surprised that there were still deliveries. Julia's voice came from the other side of the doors. I said who it was. She seemed delighted. "You came back. This is wonderful. She's been in such a bad way." I felt as if, unknowingly, I had reaffirmed Julia's faith in the entire human race. Some of us have such a terrible desire for a decent world that we will clutch at the tiniest strand of evidence for its existence and reject all other proof to the contrary. Julia looked tired. Her hair was disordered.

I unbuttoned my light raincoat and handed it to her. I pushed my suitcase under a small table which sat against the wall of the entrance hall.

"Honour went back to Flagstaff," said Julia. She looked rueful. "Just as well. She didn't think a lot of you."

"I enjoyed her candour," I said.

The woman knew I had arrived but she continued to sit at the easel we had erected together in the large front room. Light fell on a half-finished landscape, on her thinning, ash-blonde hair, on her pastel skin. She was more delicate, more beautiful, yet still I checked myself against the sensation of love for her.

"Why are you here?" She spoke in a low voice. She began to turn, resisting hope, looking at me as if I might wound her afresh. "The War isn't over."

I gestured with the newspaper. "Apparently not."

"This is too much," she said.

I told her that I had decided to take a leave. Nobody but my chief knew where I was and he had made up some story about my need to go underground with a group of radical pacifists.

"Your people won't believe that."

"Our structure is so rigid it can be resisted only by the most audacious means," I said, "and then often very successfully. It is probably one of the few advantages of orthodoxy."

"You're full of bullshit, as ever," she said. "You can't do what you did to me a second time. I'd kill myself."

I moved close to her so that my chest was on a level with her lovely head. We did not embrace. She did not look as grey or as drawn as she had when she had first been given confirmation of her illness. As she looked up at me I was impressed with her gentle beauty. She was at once noble and pathetic. Her eyes began to fill with tears. One fell. She apologised. I told her there was no need. I touched her shoulder, her cheek. She began to speak my name several times, holding tightly to my hand.

"You don't look well," she said. "You were afraid you would go crazy, weren't you?"

"I am not going to go mad," I told her. "I often wish that I could. Yet this state of control is a kind of madness, isn't it? Perhaps more profoundly insane than any other kind. But it has none of the appeal of irresponsibility, of giving up any sense of others, which the classic lunatic experiences." I laughed. "So it has no advantages."

"What about your duty?"

"To the War?"

"Or your cause, or whatever."

"Excellent excuses."

"What's more important?"

I drew a breath. "I don't know. Affection?"

"You've changed your mind. Your rationale. Your logic."

"I had to simplify."

"Now?"

"I am defeated. I can no longer maintain it. Things remain as perplexing as ever."

"What are you saying?"

I shrugged. "Love conquers all?"

"Not you!" She shook her head.

"I do not know," I said, "what the truth is. It has been my duty to lie and to counter lies. Duty allows this, demands it. The only other truth for me is the truth of my feelings, my cravings, and senses. Anything else is hypocrisy, self-deception. At best it is a sentimental rationale. We are all moved by self-interest."

"But sometimes self-interest takes on a broader form," she said. "And that is when we become human. Why are you here?"

"To see you. To be with you."

"We'll lie down," she said. "We'll go to bed."

The bed was very large. The place had belonged to her parents. Now they were in Iowa where they believed themselves to be safer. We undressed and I took her in my arms. We kissed. Her body was warm and still strong. We did not make love, but talked, as we always had. I told her that I did not know the meaning of love and that what had brought me back to her was a sense that the alternatives were less tolerable to me. I told her that a mixture of sentimentality and power politics had been the nearest substitute for love I had been able to afford in my circumstances. Altruism was a luxury. She said that she believed it a necessity. Without altruism there was no virtue in human existence, therefore if one rejected it one also rejected the only rationale for the race's continuation. Could that be why I was now on leave from the War?

I praised her for her fine fundamentalism and said that I regretted my inability to live according to such principles. She told me that it was not difficult: one did not take extra responsibility—one relinquished power and in doing that one also relinquished guilt. The very idea, I told her humorously, was terrifying to the Russian soul. Without guilt there was no movement at all! She shook her head at what she called my cynicism, my self-contempt. I said that I preferred to think I had my own measure.

I got out of bed and went into the hall. From my bag I took a pendant I had bought for her in Maracaibo. I came back and presented it to her. She looked at it and thanked me bleakly. She set it aside. "You'll never be free, then?" she said. "I believe not," I said. It was too late for that.

She rose and put on a robe, walking with her hands folded beneath her breast into the room she used as a studio. "Love and art wither without freedom." She stared at a half-finished portrait stacked against the wall. I seemed much older in the picture. "I suppose so," I said. But I was in the business of politics which, by definition, was opposed both to lovers and to artists. They were factors which always would over-complicate the game and cause enormous frustrations in those of us who preferred, by temperament, to simplify the world as much as possible.

"You've always found my reasoning stupidly romantic, haven't you?" she said. She discredited my intelligence, I said. We lived in a world of power and manipulation. Currently political decisions (I took her hand) decided if we should live or die—if we should love or create art. My realism, I said, was limited to the situation; hers was appropriate to her life as an artist and as an individual who must continue to hope. "But I am dying," she said. "I have no need for hope." She smiled as she completed the sentence. She turned away with a shrug which had much of her old gaiety in it. She ran her hands over the frames of the canvases. "I wish my life to have had some point, of course."

I could not answer her, yet suddenly I was lost in her again, as I had been during the early days of our affair. I went towards her and I embraced her. I kissed her. She recognised my emotion at once. She responded. There was a great generosity in her, a kindness. I could not at that moment bear to think of its leaving the world. But I should have a memory of it, I thought.

I told her that I admired her tendency to ascribe altruistic motives to me, to all other people. But most of us were far too selfish. We had to survive in a cynical world. She said that she had to believe in self-sufficiency and altruism was the only way by which we could, with any meaning, survive at all. One had to keep one's eye on the world as it was and somehow learn to trust oneself to maintain tolerance and hope. I said her courage was greater than mind. She acknowledged this. She said that a woman found it necessary to discover courage if she were to make any sense of her life as an individual. "But you pursued me," I said gently. "I love you," she said. "I want you for myself and will do everything I can to keep you."

"I cannot change."

"I would not wish it."

"You have won me."

"Well," she said, "I have won something of you and for the time being am content. Have I won it honourably do you think? Did you return simply out of pity."

"I was drawn here, to you. I have no reservations."

"You don't feel trapped?"

"On the contrary."

"You'll stay here?"

"Until you die."

"It might be—I might ask you to kill me when the worst begins."

"I know."

"Could you?"

"I suspect you were attracted to me because you knew that I could."

She became relieved. The tension between us vanished completely. She smiled at me and took my hand again: in love with her executioner.

(Los Angeles, August 1979,
Ladbroke Grove, March 1980)

Crossing into Cambodia

I APPROACHED AND Savitsky, Commander of the Sixth Division, got up. As usual I was impressed by his gigantic, perfect body. Yet he seemed unconscious either of his power or of his elegance. Although not obliged to do so, I almost saluted him. He stretched an arm towards me. I put the papers into his gloved hand. "These were the last messages we received," I said. The loose sleeve of his Cossack cherkesska slipped back to reveal a battle-strengthened forearm, brown and glowing. I compared his skin to my own. For all that I had ridden with the Sixth for five months, I was still pale; still possessed, I thought, of an intellectual's hands. Evening light fell through the jungle foliage and a few parrots shrieked their last goodnight. Mosquitoes were gathering in the shadows, whirling in tight-woven patterns, like a frightened mob. The jungle smelled of rot. Yakovlev, somewhere, began to play a sad accordion tune.

The Vietnamese spy we had caught spoke calmly from the other side of Savitsky's camp table. "I think I should like to be away from here before nightfall. Will you keep your word, sir, if I tell you what I know?"

Savitsky looked back and I saw the prisoner for the first time (though his presence was of course well known to the camp). His wrists and ankles were pinned to the ground with bayonets but he was otherwise unhurt.

Savitsky drew in his breath and continued to study the documents I had brought him. Our radio was now useless. "He seems to be confirming what these say." He tapped the second sheet. "An attack tonight."

The temple on the other side of the clearing came to life within. Pale light rippled on greenish, half-ruined stonework. Some of our men must have lit a fire there. I heard noises of delight and some complaints from two of the women who had been with the spy. One began to shout in that peculiar, irritating high-pitched half-wail they all use when they are trying to appeal to us. For a moment Savitsky and I had a bond in our disgust. I felt flattered. Savitsky made an impatient gesture as if of embarrassment. He turned his handsome face and looked gravely down at the peasant. "Does it matter to you? You've lost a great deal of blood."

"I do not think I am dying."

Savitsky nodded. He was economical in everything, even his cruelties. He had been prepared to tear the man apart with horses, but he knew that he would tire two already over-worked beasts. He picked up his cap from the camp table and put it thoughtfully on his head. From the deserted huts came the smell of our horses as the wind reversed its direction. I drew my borrowed burka about me. I was the only one in our unit to bother to wear it, for I felt the cold as soon as the sun was down.

"Will you show me on the map where they intend to ambush us?"

"Yes," said the peasant. "Then you can send a man to spy on their camp. He will confirm what I say."

I stood to one side while these two professionals conducted their business. Savitsky strode over to the spy and very quickly, like a man plucking a hen, drew the bayonets out and threw them on the ground. With some gentleness, he helped the peasant to his feet and sat him down in the leather campaign chair he had carried with him on our long ride from Danang, where we had disembarked off the troop-ship which had brought us from Vladivostock.

"I'll get some rags to stop him bleeding," I said.

Michael Moorcock

"Good idea," confirmed Savitsky. "We don't want the stuff all over the maps. You'd better be in on this, anyway."

As the liaison officer, it was my duty to know what was happening. That is why I am able to tell this story. My whole inclination was to return to my billet where two miserable ancients cowered and sang at me whenever I entered or left but where at least I had a small barrier between me and the casual day-to-day terrors of the campaign. But, illiterate and obtuse though these horsemen were, they had accurate instincts and could tell immediately if I betrayed any sign of fear. Perhaps, I thought, it is because they are all so used to disguising their own fears. Yet bravery was a habit with them and I yearned to catch it. I had ridden with them in more than a dozen encounters, helping to drive the Cambodians back into their own country. Each time I had seen men and horses blown to pieces, torn apart, burned alive. I had come to exist on the smell of blood and gun-powder as if it were a substitute for air and food—I identified it with the smell of Life itself—yet I had still failed to achieve that strangely passive sense of inner calm my comrades all, to a greater or lesser degree, displayed. Only in action did they seem possessed in any way by the outer world, although they still worked with efficient ferocity, killing as quickly as possible with lance, sabre or carbine and, with ghastly humanity, never leaving a wounded man of their own or the enemy's without his throat cut or a bullet in his brain. I was thankful that these, my traditional foes, were now allies for I could not have resisted them had they turned against me.

I bound the peasant's slender wrists and ankles. He was like a child. He said: "I knew there were no arteries cut." I nodded at him. "You're the political officer, aren't you?" He spoke almost rympathetically.

"Liaison," I said.

He was satisfied by my reply, as if I had confirmed his opinion. He added: "I suppose it's the leather coat. Almost a uniform."

I smiled. "A sign of class difference, you think?"

His eyes were suddenly drowned with pain and he staggered, but recovered to finish what he had evidently planned to say: "You Russians are natural bourgeoisie. It's not your fault. It's your turn."

Savitsky was too tired to respond with anything more than a

small smile. I felt that he agreed with the peasant and that these two excluded me, felt superior to me. I knew anger, then. Tightening the last rag on his left wrist, I made the spy wince. Satisfied that my honour was avenged I cast an eye over the map. "Here we are," I said. We were on the very edge of Cambodia. A small river, easily forded, formed the border. We had heard it just before we had entered this village. Scouts confirmed that it lay no more than half a verst to the west. The stream on the far side of the village, behind the temple, was a tributary.

"You give your word you won't kill me," said the Vietnamese.

"Yes," said Savitsky. He was beyond joking. We all were. It had been ages since any of us had been anything but direct with one another, save for the conventional jests which were merely part of the general noise of the squadron, like the jangling of harness. And he was beyond lying, except where it was absolutely necessary. His threats were as unqualified as his promises.

"They are here." The spy indicated a town. He began to shiver. He was wearing only torn shorts. "And some of them are here, because they think you might use the bridge rather than the ford."

"And the attacking force for tonight?"

"Based here." A point on our side of the river.

Savitsky shouted. "Pavlichenko."

From the Division Commander's own tent, young Pavlichenko, capless, with ruffled fair hair and a look of restrained disappointment, emerged. "Comrade?"

"Get a horse and ride with this man for half-an-hour the way we came today. Ride as fast as you can, then leave him and return to camp."

Pavlichenko ran towards the huts where the horses were stabled. Savitsky had believed the spy and was not bothering to check his information. "We can't attack them," he murmured. "We'll have to wait until they come to us. It's better." The flap of Savitsky's tent was now open. I glanced through and to my surprise saw a Eurasian girl of about fourteen. She had her feet in a bucket of water. She smiled at me. I looked away.

Savitsky said: "He's washing her for me. Pavlichenko's an expert."

"My wife and daughters?" said the spy.

"They'll have to remain now. What can I do?" Savitsky shrugged in the direction of the temple. "You should have spoken earlier."

The Vietnamese accepted this and, when Pavlichenko returned with the horse, leading it and running as if he wished to get the job over with in the fastest possible time, he allowed the young Cossack to lift him onto the saddle.

"Take your rifle," Savitsky told Pavlichenko. "We're expecting an attack."

Pavlichenko dashed for his own tent, the small one close to Savitsky's. The horse, as thoroughly trained as the men who rode him, stood awkwardly but quietly beneath his nervous load. The spy clutched the saddle pommel, the mane, his bare feet angled towards the mount's neck. He stared ahead of him into the night. His wife and daughter had stopped their appalling wailing but I thought I could hear the occasional feminine grunt from the temple. The flames had become more animated. His other daughter, her feet still in the bucket, held her arms tightly under her chest and her curious eyes looked without rancour at her father, then at the Division Commander, then, finally, at me. Savitsky spoke. "You're the intellectual. She doesn't know Russian. Tell her that her father will be safe. She can join him tomorrow."

"My Vietnamese might not be up to that."

"Use English or French, then." He began to tidy his maps, calling over Kreshenko, who was in charge of the guard.

I entered the tent and was shocked by her little smile. She had a peculiar smell to her—like old tea and cooked rice. I knew my Vietnamese was too limited so I asked her if she spoke French. She was of the wrong generation. "Amerikanski," she told me. I relayed Savitsky's message. She said: "So I am the price of the old bastard's freedom."

"Not at all." I reassured her. "He told us what we wanted. It was just bad luck for you that he used you three for cover."

She laughed. "Nuts! It was me got him to do it. With my sister. Tao's boyfriend works for the Cambodians." She added: "They seemed to be winning at the time."

Savitsky entered the tent and zipped it up from the bottom.

He used a single, graceful movement. For all that he was bone-weary, he moved with the unconscious fluidity of an acrobat. He lit one of his foul-smelling papyrosi and sat heavily on the camp bed beside the girl.

"She speaks English," I said. "She's a half-caste. Look."

He loosened his collar. "Could you ask her if she's clean, comrade?"

"I doubt it," I said. I repeated what she had told me.

He nodded. "Well, ask her if she'll be a good girl and use her mouth. I just want to get on with it. I expect she does, too."

I relayed the D.C.'s message.

"I'll bite his cock off if I get the chance," said the girl.

Outside in the night the horse began to move away. I explained what she had said.

"I wonder, comrade," Savitsky said, "if you would oblige me by holding the lady's head." He began to undo the belt of his trousers, pulling up his elaborately embroidered shirt.

The girl's feet became noisy in the water and the bucket overturned. In my leather jacket, my burka, with my automatic pistol at her right ear, I restrained the girl until Savitsky had finished with her. He began to take off his boots. "Would you care for her, yourself?"

I shook my head and escorted the girl from the tent. She was walking in that familiar stiff way women have after they have been raped. I asked her if she was hungry. She agreed that she was. I took her to my billet. The old couple found some more rice and I watched her eat it.

Later that night she moved towards me from where she had been lying more or less at my feet. I thought I was being attacked and shot her in the stomach. Knowing what my comrades would think of me if I tried to keep her alive (it would be a matter of hours) I shot her in the head to put her out of her misery. As luck would have it, these shots woke the camp and when the Khmer soldiers attacked a few moments later we were ready for them and killed a great many before the rest ran back into the jungle. Most of these soldiers were younger than the girl.

In the morning, to save any embarrassment, the remaining women were chased out of the camp in the direction taken by the patriarch. The old couple had disappeared and I assumed that they would not return or, if they did, that they would bury the girl, so I left her where I had shot her. A silver ring she wore would compensate them for their trouble. There was very little food remaining in the village, but what there was we ate for our breakfast or packed into our saddle-bags. Then, mounting up, we followed the almost preturnaturally handsome Savitsky back into the jungle, heading for the river.

II

WHEN OUR SCOUT did not return after we had heard a long burst of machine-gun fire, we guessed that he had found at least part of the enemy ambush and that the spy had not lied to us, so we decided to cross the river at a less convenient spot where, with luck, no enemy would be waiting.

The river was swift but had none of the force of Russian rivers and Pavlichenko was sent across with a rope which he tied to a tree-trunk. Then we entered the water and began to swim our horses across. Those who had lost the canvas covers for their carbines kept them high in the air, holding the rope with one hand and guiding their horses with legs and with reins which they gripped in their teeth. I was more or less in the middle, with half the division behind me and half beginning to assemble on dry land on the other side, when Cambodian aircraft sighted us and began to attack dive. The aircraft were in poor repair, borrowed from half-a-dozen other countries, and their guns, aiming equipment and, I suspect, their pilots, were in worse condition, but they killed seven of our men as we let go of the ropes, slipped out of our saddles, and began to swim beside our horses, making for the far bank, while those still on dry land behind us went to cover where they could. A couple of machine-gun carts were turned on the attacking planes, but these were of little use. the peculiar assortment of weapons used against us—tracers, two rockets, a few napalm canisters which struck the water and sank (only one opened and burned but the mixture was quickly carried off by the current) and then they were flying back to base somewhere in Cambodia's interior—indicated that they had very little conventional armament left. This was true of most of the participants at this stage, which is why our cavalry had proved so effective. But they had bought some time for their ground-troops who were now coming in.

In virtual silence, any shouts drowned by the rushing of the river, we crossed to the enemy bank and set up a defensive position, using the machine-gun carts which were last to come across on ropes. The Cambodians hit us from two sides—moving in from their original ambush positions—but we were able to return their fire effectively, even using the anti-tank weapons and the mortar which, hitherto, we had tended to consider useless weight. They used arrows, blow-darts, automatic rifles, pistols and a flame-thrower which only worked for a few seconds and did us no harm. The Cossacks were not happy with this sort of warfare and as soon as there was a lull we had mounted up, packed the gear in the carts, and with sabres drawn were howling into the Khmer Stalinists (as we had been instructed to term them). Leaving them scattered and useless, we found a bit of concrete road along which we could gallop for a while. We slowed to a trot and then to a walk, as the pavement was potholed and only slightly less dangerous than the jungle floor. The jungle was behind us now and seemed to have been a screen hiding the devastation ahead. The landscape was virtually flat, as if it had been bombed clean of contours, with a few broken buildings, the occasional blackened tree, and ash drifted across the road, coming sometimes up to our horses' knees. The ash was stirred by a light wind. We had witnessed scenes like it before, but never on such a scale. The almost colourless nature of the landscape was emphasised by the unrelieved brilliance of the blue sky overhead. The sun had become very hot.

Once we saw two tanks on the horizon, but they did not challenge us. We continued until early afternoon when we came to the remains of some sort of modern power installation and we made camp in the shelter of its walls. The ash got into our food and we drank more of our water than was sensible. We were all covered in the grey stuff by this time.

"We're like corpses," said Savitsky. He resembled an heroic statue of the sort which used to be found in almost every public square in the Soviet Union. "Where are we going to find anything to eat in this?"

"It's like the end of the world," I said.

"Have you tried the radio again?"

I shook my head. "It isn't worth it. Napalm eats through wiring faster than it easts through you."

He accepted this and with a naked finger began to clean off the inner rims of the goggles he (like most of us) wore as protection against sun, rain and dust. "I could do with some orders," he said.

"We were instructed to move into the enemy's territory. That's what we're doing."

"Where, we were told, we would link up with American and Australian mounted units. Those fools can't ride. I don't know why they ever thought of putting them on horses. Cowboys!"

I saw no point in repeating an already stale argument. It was true, however, that the Western cavalry divisions found it hard to match our efficient savagery. I had been amused, too, when they had married us briefly with a couple of Mongolian squadrons. The Mongols had not ridden to war in decades and had become something of a laughing stock with their ancient enemies, the Cossacks. Savitsky believed that we were the last great horsemen. Actually, he did not include me, for I was a very poor rider and not a Cossack, anyway. He thought it was our destiny to survive the War and begin a new and braver civilisation: "Free from the influence of women and Jews". He recalled the great days of the Zaporozhian Sech, from which women had been forbidden. Even amongst the Sixth he was regarded as something of a conservative. He continued to be admired more than his opinions.

When the men had watered our horses and replaced the water bags in the cart, Savitsky and I spread the map on a piece of concrete and found our position with the help of the compass and sextant (there were no signs or landmarks). "I wonder what has happened to Angkor," I said. It was where we were supposed to meet other units, including the Canadians to whom, in the months to come, I was to be attached (I was to discover later that they had been in our rear all along).

"You think it's like this?" Savitsky gestured. His noble eyes began to frown. "I mean, comrade, would you say it was worth our while making for Angkor now?"

"We have our orders," I said. "We've no choice. We're expected."

Savitsky blew dust from his mouth and scratched his head. "There's about half our division left. We could do with reinforcements. Mind you, I'm glad we can see a bit of sky at last." We had all felt claustrophobic in the jungle.

"What is it, anyway, this Angkor? Their capital?" he asked me.

"Their Stalingrad, maybe."

Savitsky understood. "Oh, it has an importance to their morale. It's not strategic?"

"I haven't been told about its strategic value."

Savitsky, as usual, withdrew into his diplomatic silence, indicating that he did not believe me and thought that I had been instructed to secrecy. "We'd best push on," he said. "We've a long way to go, eh?"

After we had mounted up, Savitsky and I rode side by side for a while, along the remains of the concrete road. We were some way ahead of the long column, with its riders, its baggage-waggons, and its Makhno-style machine-gun carts. We were sitting targets for any planes and, because there was no cover, Savitsky and his men casually ignored the danger. I had learned not to show my nervousness but I was not at that moment sure how well hidden it was.

"We are the only vital force in Cambodia," said the Division Commander with a beatific smile. "Everything else is dead. How these yellow bastards must hate one another." He was impressed, perhaps admiring.

"Who's to say?" I ventured. "We don't know who else has been fighting. There isn't a nation now that's not in the War."

"And not one that's not on its last legs. Even Switzerland." Savitsky gave a superior snort. "But what an inheritance for us!"

I became convinced that, quietly, he was going insane.

III

WE CAME ACROSS an armoured car in a hollow, just off the road. One of our scouts had heard the crew's moans. As Savitsky and I rode up, the scout was covering the uniformed Khmers with his carbine, but they were too far gone to offer us any harm.

"What's wrong with 'em," Savitsky asked the scout.

The scout did not know. "Disease," he said. "Or starvation.

They're not wounded."

We got off our horses and slid down into the crater. The car was undamaged. It appeared to have rolled gently into the dust and become stuck. I slipped into the driving seat and tried to start the engine, but it was dead. Savitsky had kicked one of the wriggling Khmers in the genitals but the man did not seem to notice the pain much, though he clutched himself, almost as if he entered into the spirit of a ritual. Savitsky was saying 'Soldiers. Soldiers', over and over again. It was one of the few Vietnamese words he knew. He pointed in different directions, looking with disgust on the worn-out men. "You'd better question them," he said to me.

They understood my English, but refused to speak it. I tried them in French. "What happened to your machine?"

The man Savitsky had kicked continued to lie on his face, his arms stretched along the ashy ground towards us. I felt he wanted to touch us: to steal our vitality. I felt sick as I put the heel of my boot on his hand. One of his comrades said: "There's no secret to it. We ran out of essence." He pointed to the armoured car. "We ran out of essence."

"You're a long way from your base."

"Our base is gone. There's no essence anywhere."

I believed him and told Savitsky who was only too ready to accept this simple explanation.

As usual, I was expected to dispatch the prisoners. I reached for my holster, but Savitsky, with rare sympathy, stayed my movement. "Go and see what's in that can," he said, pointing. As I waded towards the punctured metal, three shots came from the Division Commander's revolver. I wondered at his mercy. Continuing with this small farce, I looked at the can, held it up, shook it, and threw it back into the dust. "Empty," I said.

Savitsky was climbing the crater towards his horse. As I scrambled behind him he said: "It's the Devil's world. Do you think we should give ourselves up to Him?"

I was astonished by this unusual cynicism.

He got into his saddle. Unconsciously, he assumed the pose, often seen in films and pictures, of the noble revolutionary horseman—his head lifted, his palm shielding his eyes as he peered towards the West.

"We seem to have wound up killing Tatars again," he said

with a smile as I got clumsily onto my horse. "Do you believe in all this History, comrade?"

"I've always considered the theory of precedent absolutely infantile," I said.

"What's that?"

I began to explain, but he was already spurring forward, shouting to his men.

IV

ON THE THIRD day we had passed through the ash-desert and our horses could at last crop at some grass on the crest of a line of low hills which looked down on glinting, misty paddy-fields. Savitsky, his field-glasses to his eyes, was relieved. "A village," he said. "Thank god. We'll be able to get some provisions."

"And some exercise," said Pavlichenko behind him. The boy laughed, pushing his cap back on his head and wiping grimey sweat from his brow. "Shall I go down there, comrade?"

Savitsky agreed, telling Pavlichenko to take two others with him. We watched the Cossacks ride down the hill and begin cautiously to wade their horses through the young rice. The sky possessed a greenish tinge here, as if it reflected the fields. It looked like the Black Sea lagoons at midsummer. A smell of foliage, almost shocking in its unfamiliarity, floated up to us. Savitsky was intent on watching the movements of his men, who had unslung their carbines and dismounted as they reached the village. With reins looped on their arms they moved slowly in, firing a few experimental rounds at the huts. One of them took a dummy grenade from his saddle-bag and threw it into a nearby doorway. Peasants, already starving to the point of death it seemed, ran out. The young Cossacks ignored them, looking for soldiers. When they were satisfied that the village was clear of traps, they waved us in. The peasants began to gather together at the centre of the village. Evidently they were used to this sort of operation.

While our men made their thorough search I was again called upon to perform my duty and question the inhabitants. These, it emerged, were almost all intellectuals, part of one of the Khmer Rouge re-education programmes (virtually a sentence of death by forced labour). It was easier to speak to them but harder to understand their complicated answers. In the end I gave up and, made impatient by the whining appeals of the wretches, ignored them. They knew nothing of use to us. Our men were disappointed in their expectations. There were only old people in the village. In the end they took the least aged of the women off and had them in what had once been some sort of administration hut. I wondered at their energy. It occurred to me that this was something they expected of one another and that they would lose face if they did not perform the necessary actions. Eventually, when we had eaten what we could find, I returned to questioning two of the old men. They were at least antagonistic to the Cambodian troops and were glad to tell us anything they could. However, it seemed there had been no large movements in the area. The occasional plane or helicopter had gone over a few days earlier. These were probably part of the flight which had attacked us at the river. I asked if they had any news of Angkor, but there was no radio here and they expected us to know more than they did. I pointed towards the purple hills on the other side of the valley. "What's over there?"

They told me that as far as they knew it was another valley, similar to this but larger. The hills looked steeper and were wooded. It would be a difficult climb for us unless there was a road. I got out the map. There was a road indicated. I pointed to it. One of the old men nodded. Yes, he thought that road was still there, for it led, eventually, to this village. He showed me where the path was. It was rutted where, some time earlier, heavy vehicles had been driven along it. It disappeared into dark, green, twittering jungle. All the jungle meant to me now was mosquitoes and a certain amount of cover from attacking planes.

Careless of leeches and insects, the best part of the division was taking the chance of a bath in the stream which fed the paddy-fields. I could not bring myself to strip in the company of these healthy men. I decided to remain dirty until I had the chance of some sort of privacy.

"I want the men to rest," said Savitsky. "Have you any objection to our camping here for the rest of today and tonight?"

"It's a good idea," I said. I sought out a hut, evicted the occupants, and went almost immediately to sleep.

In the morning I was awakened by a trooper who brought me a metal mug full of the most delicately scented tea. I was astonished and accepted it with some amusement. "There's loads of it here," he said. "It's all they've got!"

I sipped the tea. I was still in my uniform, with the burka on the ground beneath me and my leather jacket folded for a pillow. The hut was completely bare. I was used to seeing a few personal possessions and began to wonder if they had hidden their stuff when they had seen us coming. Then I remembered that they were from the towns and had been brought here forcibly. Perhaps now, I thought, the war would pass them by and they would know peace, even happiness, for a bit. I was scratching my ear and stretching when Savitsky came in, looking grim. "We've found a damned burial ground," he said. "Hundreds of bodies in a pit. I think they must be the original inhabitants. And one or two soldiers—at least, they were in uniform."

"You want me to ask what they are?"

"No! I just want to get away. God knows what they've been doing to one another. They're a filthy race. All grovelling and secret killing. They've no guts."

"No soldiers, either," I said. "Not really. They've been preyed on by bandits for centuries. Bandits are pretty nearly the only sort of soldiers they've ever known. So the ones who want to be soldiers emulate them. Those who don't want to be soldiers treat the ones who do as they've always treated bandits. They are conciliatory until they get a chance to turn the tables."

He was impressed by this. He rubbed at a freshly-shaven chin. He looked years younger, though he still had the monumental appearance of a god. "Thieves, you mean. They have the mentality of thieves, their soldiers?"

"Aren't the Cossacks thieves?"

"That's not foraging." He was not angry. Very little I said could ever anger him because he had no respect for my opinions. I was the necessary political officer, his only link with the higher, distant authority of the Kremlin, but he did not have to respect my ideas any more than he respected those which came to him from Moscow. What he respected there was the power and the fact that in some way Russia was mystically represented in our leaders. "We leave in ten minutes," he said.

I noticed that Pavlichenko had polished his boots for him.

By that afternoon, after we had crossed the entire valley on an excellent dirt road through the jungle and had reached the top of the next range of hills, I had a pain in my stomach. Savitsky noticed me holding my hands against my groin and said laconically, "I wish the doctor hadn't been killed. Do you think it's typhus?" Naturally, it was what I had suspected.

"I think it's just the tea and the rice and the other stuff. Maybe mixing with all the dust we've swallowed." He looked paler than usual. "I've got it, too. So have half the others. Oh, shit!"

It was hard to tell, in that jungle at that time of day, if you had a fever. I decided to put the problem out of my mind as much as possible until sunset when it would become cooler.

The road began to show signs of damage and by the time we were over the hill and looking down on the other side we were confronting scenery if anything more desolate than that which we had passed through on the previous three days. It was a grey desert, scarred by the broken road and bomb-craters. Beyond this and coming towards us was a wall of dark dust; unmistakably an army on the move. Savitsky automatically relaxed in his saddle and turned back to see our men moving slowly up the wooded hill. "I think they must be heading this way." Savitsky cocked his head to one side. "What's that?"

It was a distant shriek. Then a whole squadron of planes was coming in low. We could see their crudely-painted Khmer Rouge markings, their battered fuselages. There were half-a-dozen different types of jet in the squadron. The men began to scatter off the road, but the planes ignored us. They went zooming by, seeming to be fleeing rather than attacking. I looked at the sky, but nothing followed them.

We took our field-glasses from their cases and adjusted them. In the dust I saw a mass of barefoot infantry bearing rifles with fixed bayonets. There were also trucks, a few tanks, some private cars, bicycles, motor-bikes, ox-carts, hand-carts, civilians with bundles. It was an orgy of defeated soldiers and refugees.

"I think we've missed the action." Savitsky was furious. "We were beaten to it, eh? And by Australians, probably!"

My impulse to shrug was checked. "Damn!" I said a little weakly.

This caused Savitsky to laugh at me. "You're relieved. Admit it!"

I knew that I dare not share his laughter, lest it become hysterical and turn to tears, so I missed a moment of possible comradeship. "What shall we do?" I asked. "Go round them?"

"It would be easy enough to go through them. Finish them off. It would stop them destroying this valley, at least." He did not, by his tone, much care.

The men were assembling behind us. Savitsky informed them of the nature of the rabble ahead of us. He put his field-glasses to his eyes again and said to me: "Infantry, too. Quite a lot. Coming on faster."

I looked. The barefoot soldiers were apparently pushing their way through the refugees to get ahead of them.

"Maybe the planes radioed back," said Savitsky. "Well, it's something to fight."

"I think we should go round," I said. "We should save our strength. We don't know what's waiting for us at Angkor."

"It's miles away yet."

"Our instructions were to avoid any conflict we could," I reminded him.

He sighed. "This is Satan's own country." He was about to give the order which would comply with my suggestion when, from the direction of Angkor Wat, the sky burst into white fire. The horses reared and whinneyed. Some of our men yelled and flung their arms over their eyes. We were all temporarily blinded. Then the dust below seemed to grow denser and denser. We watched in fascination as the dark wall became taller, rushing upon us and howling like a million dying voices. We were struck by the ash and forced onto our knees, then onto our bellies, yanking our frightened horses down with us as best we could. The stuff stung my face and hands and even those parts of my body protected by heavy clothing. Larger pieces of stone rattled against my goggles.

When the wind had passed and we began to stand erect, the sky was still very bright. I was astonished that my field glasses were intact. I put them up to my burning eyes and peered through swirling ash at the Cambodians. The army was running along the road towards us, as terrified animals flee a forest-fire. I knew now what the planes had been escaping. Our Cossacks were in some confusion, but were already regrouping, shouting amonst themselves. A number of horses were still shying and whickering but by and large we were all calm again.

"Well, comrade," said Savitsky with a sort of mad satisfaction, "what do we do now? Wasn't that Angkor Wat, where we're supposed to meet our allies?"

I was silent. The mushroom cloud on the horizon was growing. It had the hazy outlines of a gigantic, spreading cedar tree, as if all at once that wasteland of ash had become promiscuously fertile. An aura of bloody red seemed to surround it, like a silhouette in the sunset.

The strong, artificial wind was still blowing in our direction. I wiped dust from my goggles and lowered them back over my eyes. Savitsky gave the order for our men to mount. "Those bastards down there are in our way," he said. "We're going to charge them."

"What?" I could not believe him.

"When in doubt," he told me, "attack."

"You're not scared of the enemy," I said, "but there's the radiation."

"I don't know anything about radiation." He turned in his saddle to watch his men. When they were ready he drew his sabre. The imitated him. I had no sabre to draw.

I was horrified. I pulled my horse away from the road. "Division Commander Savitsky, we're duty-bound to conserve..."

"We're duty-bound to make for Angkor," he said. "And that's what we're doing." His perfect body poised itself in the saddle, He raised his sabre.

"It's not like ordinary dying," I began. But he gave the order and began to trot forward. The men followed. There was a rictus of terrifying glee on each mouth. The light from the sky was reflected in every eye.

I moved with them. I had become used to the security of numbers and I could not face their disapproval. But gradually they went ahead of me until I was in the rear. By this time we were almost at the bottom of the hill and trotting towards the mushroom cloud which was now shot through with all kinds of dark, swirling colours. It had become like a threatening hand, while the wind-borne ash stung our bodies and drew blood on the flanks of our mounts.

Yakovlev, just ahead of me, unstrapped his accordion and began to play some familiar Cossack battle-song. Soon they were all singing. Their pace gradually increased. The noise of the accordion died but their song was so loud now that it seemed to fill the whole world. They reached full gallop, charging upon that appalling outline, the quintessential symbol of our doom, as their ancestors might have charged the very gates of Hell. They were swift, dark shapes in the dust. The song became a savage, defiant roar.

My first impulse was to charge with them. But then I had turned my horse and was trotting back towards the valley and the border, praying that, if I ever got to safety, I would not be too badly contaminated.

THE END

(In homage to Isaac Babel, 1894-1941?)

Ladbroke Grove, 1978

Two

The Dodgem Division

1.

IT WAS NOT their accomplishments that Jerry disliked so much as their attitudes. It had been such a mark of English literature, certainly since Chesterton. It was traceable in all the donnish 'novels' and detective stories, the fantasies of people like Tolkien, Williams and Lewis, the work of self-styled 'poets' like Conquest and Mitchell, the music of Vaughan Williams and Eric Coates, reaching its final depths in the ill-constructed, soft-minded concoctions of John Braine, Kingsley Amis and the rest.

An attitude of mind.

Just as the harmonium corrupted Indian classical music, so had the operettas of Gilbert and Sullivan subtly corroded the quality of English thinking. Attitudes that aimed at reinforcing opinions rather than analysing them, at preserving conventions rather than expanding them.

Pints of beer in the good old English pub. Jolly jokes in the senior common room. The most that a novel can hope to be is an amusing pastiche or a work of sociology. Even a light comic narrative became a 'protest', a piece of melodramatic wish-fulfilment became 'an indictment of society', and a bit of conventional stream-of-consciousness became 'experimental'.

2.

DRIVING THE PHANTOM VI along the front at Brighton, Jerry looked out to sea. It was inescapable, he thought. It was large. It could not be comfortably dealt with. It was a fact. An old woman staggered out into the road in front of his car. Another fact. He didn't stop, hardly noticing the bump.

3.

HE REFLECTED ON the desperate search for a label, on the way in which the word Surrealism had been resurrected to stand for anything that was not a 'realistic' narrative. Most of the stuff the publishers presented under this label bore as much similarity to surrealistic texts as Ardizzone bore to Ernst. But then what was 'the new fiction' but a label? He glanced at the copy of *New Worlds* on the seat beside him. The slogan for that month read: 'What do you need?'

4.

HE HAD REACHED Hove with its bland white blocks facing not towards the sea but onto neat green squares where old women, all wool and chocolates, trailed their decrepit domestic pets and a faint smell of rotting underlinen. This, of course, was where the shopkeepers came to die, to complain that the sea didn't have enough sugar in it, to be bullied by beer-reddened newsagents and overcharged by decaying waitresses. On the whole they took it passively, as if their past lives could be redeemed by the punishments and indignities inflicted by this suburb by the sea. And yet at the same time they appeared to seek reassurance that their lives had not been useless, selfish, narrow and full of spite. Perhaps this was why they clung on to existence, (hoping that if they could live another year or two they would receive some sign) obsessively comforting their ruined bodies. To cater to this unvocalised hope there were the Health Food Shops and the *Daily*

Express. But the *Daily Express* saw itself in a humbler light, directing the pilgrims on to the revelations of James Bond, John Braine and the latest Kingsley Amis.

5.

MUSIC CRITICS WHO had praised the virtues of the Beatles had given authority to the opinions of the tone-deaf who now praised anything from the Electric String Band to The Doors. A similar process, where the virtues of Kipling and Chesterton were praised, had made it possible for all those critics whose bad taste encompassed anything from Ian Fleming to Kingsley Amis to praise the books and get away with it. Such critics recognised similar attitudes in the writers they admired and so assumed them to have the talent and craftsmanship of their predecessors.

It's the rambling English drunkard who made the rambling English narrative, thought Jerry, completing the U-turn and driving back towards the West Pier. And it was left to Leavis to confuse intellectual rigour with moral rigour, to mistake, in the final analysis, fiction for sociology. What's it about, then? Symbolism was a stale joke. There was no substitute for imagination. He passed the ambulance where they were carefully carrying an old lady on a stretcher. Things had come to a pretty pass when the work of Firbank was ignored in favour of his imitator Waugh whose prose, diffuse in comparison with that of his master, was thought to represent the best of English style; where critics sought to mine a social thesis from *No Laughing Matter* and missed the fact that, in terms of its structure and control, its range and the depth of its observation, it was one of the finest true novels in the English language, and perhaps one of the few of any stature published since Thomas Mann.

If only Connolly had heeded his own warnings; if only he had convinced contemporaries like Karl Miller and Kenneth Tynan. The muse had become a fat old lady in a bathing machine, a stern Presbyterian Scottish aunt. The schools produced nothing but anachronisms. Their revolutions were not intellectual but vaguely political and therefore boring.

There was nothing more old-fashioned than the speeches of the last members of the Old Guard, the student revolutionaries. The 20th Century Confusion.

6.

FEELING THAT HE was familiar enough with the attitudes of the Brighton authorities, he parked the Rolls Royce on a double yellow line and got out. He crossed to the promenade and looked down on the beach.

A column of constables, headed by a local magistrate with the honest stupid face of an unsuccessful used-car salesman, carefully searched the litter baskets for offensive reading matter. Each was armed with a stick of rock shaped like a walking stick, and with these they picked among the soiled copies of the *Daily Mail* and the *Sunday Telegraph*, the chip bags, the old sandwiches and the lolly wrappers. Jerry lowered his sack to the ground and opened it, throwing out copies of THE CRYING GAME, I WANT IT NOW, and MUSRUM. The constables were too immersed in their search to notice the fluttering things that hit the beach like dying crows.

7.

THE SUN SET and Jerry stayed on the dodgems as he had for the past four hours. He was badly bruised on his right knee and had grazed his hand, but the dodgems on the East Pier were among the best in the country and he wanted to make the most of them. For an hour he had been pursued by a middle-aged man in an orange car. He recognised his old friend from Burma, Captain Maxwell. He had lost weight. Jerry turned his dodgem and rammed the orange car head-on. Jarred, Captain Maxwell scowled, but did not look at Jerry. He had little sense of humour, Jerry remembered.

8.

DRIVING SLOWLY ALONG the front under the lights, Jerry wondered why there should be a need for a new fiction. Were there really new ideas circulating? New subject matter? Probably. But even if there were not, it was always better to try to extend the range of fiction. Stylistic revolution always preceded the contextual revolution and that was in progress already. Though few admitted it, the revolution was as good as accomplished. This place, he thought, heading into a side-street, it's like some Margate of the mind.

Most of the books published in England were already dead before birth. It was disgusting, really. One would have expected a certain amount of development in the field of preventive medicine. Captain Mackenzie had suggested a contraceptive on the fountain pen as a suitable remedy. That way they could scribble all day and do no harm to anyone.

Perhaps someone had suggested it first to Mackenzie?

Dead languages were taught in the universities—the languages were formal, often very beautiful, and certainly quite complex. Learning them imposed a certain necessary discipline, perhaps. But the language was no longer relevant to the present day. One might just as well attempt to produce a narrative in classical Greek in the manner of Homer. Not a bad exercise, of course, like a lot of pastiches, but hardly vital.

All the experiments in style of the first half of the century had been attempts to freshen the approach to the old concerns. Many writers of the period had abandoned them, eventually, because they had discovered that the old techniques were better suited to the old concerns. But now elements of those styles were being used as they had never been used before. He turned the car towards Lewes.

9.

AS HE CHECKED the fuses, Jerry glanced up, afraid that the moonlight had caught his silver swastika cufflinks. He had chosen them with special care. It was best to know all the implications of an action.

He backed away from the building, making his way to his parked car. As soon as he was in the Phantom VI he touched a stud on the dashboard.

Behind him there was a roar as the books went up. He stuck an arm out of the window and waved at the crowd; then he drove back to Brighton.

10.

PLEASED WITH HIS naiveté, Jerry wondered what else he could do before he left. He was so tired of debate. The facts remained. It was boring to be so explicit. It pleased nobody. He fingered the gold Star of David at his throat. How evolved everything was. It was time to be moving on.

11.

OLD MEN IN Harris Tweed sports jackets with leather patches on the elbows wandered along the asphalt talking about jazz and science fiction, about politics and even religion.

They considered their tastes and opinions to be radical, vital. It was such a shame.

Jerry Cornelius leaned against the one remaining wall of the library. Why did the establishment of any generation always consider themselves progressive? By the time they achieved power their battles were old, whether they had been won, lost or forgotten. If the policemen were getting younger, the BBC producers were getting older.

12.

THE GESTURES OF fear. The words of self-comfort. The talk of craftsmanship by those not skilled enough to construct a simple traditional narrative. The provincial philistinism that, as an act of pseudo-rebellion, was so much easier to cultivate than an informed attitude. At least, thought Jerry, Chesterton could construct a decent enough essay. He thought of *Writing in England Today* with its sad substitutes for the essay—of *The James Bond Dossier* of which the most damning thing that could be said about it was that it was not willfully bad (the only joke was Amis's reference to it as 'belles-lettres'), his particular contribution to that body of work which included a Latin translation of *Winnie the Pooh*. Cardigans, cardigans, cardigans. With their woollies and their brandy, the academics were no better or worse than the poor old ratbags dying in Hove and Worthing and Bognor Regis. Who were they fighting? Why were they running away? The bawling of opinions (Amis's review of LOLITA was as wearying as Nabokov's opinions of everything) had become the substitute for reasoned argument. It was accepted everywhere in England as a good enough substitute.

13.

LONDON DREW CLOSER and Jerry began to relax. He switched on the radio. The persistent confusion of art with politics was maddening. English critics chiefly argued with the moral attitudes they believed they discovered in works of fiction and seemed unable to discuss the qualities of the fiction. They approved of books whose moral attitude, as they saw it, they shared, disapproved of those with which they couldn't agree. Faced with books that refused to be interpreted, they dismissed them. Later academics would do worse. They would provide 'keys'.

14.

IN HIS HOUSE overlooking Holland Park, Jerry watched the autumn light as it faded. If a 'new fiction' existed, its concerns were with new ways in which a narrative could be constructed and presented, as well as with thorough familiarity with subject matter still regarded with suspicion by the older members of the establishment and by its younger members as something startling and shiny with which to pep up the old forms. Only the most recent generation of writers—chiefly American and English—were able to deal with it in a completely relaxed way, taking it for granted as they took the H-Bomb for granted, for they had grown up with it. Computers and spaceships, among other things, had been the subject matter of their childhood reading. Some contemporary fiction was now actually dealing with contemporary situations, images, events, ideas, attitudes, characters. And a little of that dealt with the subject matter in a manner that suited it. If people found the form unfamiliar, impossible to appreciate, it was perhaps because they thought the same about the stuff that the form was attempting to deal with. Most publishers, magazines, journals, were incapable of knowing what the modern public wished to read, and they blamed their falling sales on everything but their own judgement.

15.

THE DOCUMENTARY FICTION of the fifties, that still appeared in establishment magazines like *Evergreen* and so on, had been, quite evidently, the precursor of the new fiction. The documentary stuff had dealt with the subject matter but at best it was semi-fiction, dramatised reportage, excellent journalism. It had been left to a new generation to take it and apply imagination, to create a synthesis, a true form of fiction. Perhaps it would take still another generation to produce the masterpieces. But the use of the word 'generation' was too loose, Jerry thought as he opened the window to smell the smoky autumn for a good many years separated Via, Geddes, Ballard, Mathews and the rest, and their differences of approach, of course, were quite as marked as their similarities.

16.

JERRY SWITCHED ON his new light machine and tuned it to the stereo, sat down at his IBM 2000 and began to compose a book. He had planned it for 4000 words, but now it seemed it would emerge as 4,250. He hoped that the extra length would not bore the reader. He selected a 10/11pt. imitation Times for the main text and would probably not bother to justify the right hand margin. He would run off 2,000 copies at first and see how it went. If it went well he might transfer it to a strip of 35mm for a household projector or he might put it on disc. He would have to ask his distributor.

It was strange, he thought, how even a few months ago a writer could not control every stage of his work's production, that it would involve editors, publishers, agents, contracts, compositors, printers, binders, and the rest. He could remember how he had once been prepared to operate in that system. It was hard to believe how it had been possible. Now his only concern was with the efficiency of his distributor.

Hey, how does this thing work!?

17.

HISTORICAL ANALOGIES were always suspicious, Jerry thought; yet it did seem that the reportage disguised as fiction and the fiction disguised as reportage preceded the emergence of a true fiction form. But the whole subject was beginning to tire him. There were stories to write. One only produced essays when one was not actually doing the work. That was why interviews with novelists and film-makers were always misleading. Usually they only had time to give the interviews, or write the articles, between their creative patches. So they usually appeared jaundiced, tired, cynical. "It's all a con." Their work remained and it meant a great deal more than any amount of analysis by the person himself or his critics. The work was the fact. It needed no rationale. To have a positive attitude was to have at best a limited one. Live and let live, thought Jerry. But there was a time when the bastards wouldn't give me a chance.

18.

HE WATCHED THE television before he went to bed. Its red gun was misfiring and this gave the pictures of Vietnam, Biafra, Czechoslovakia, the spaceflight and the latest heart-transplant, a distinct green caste, as if everything took place under the shade of gigantic tropical trees. He switched off.

You had to think fast, read fast, write fast these days, but never hastily. It was the only way.

Maybe it was time to leave the hothouse.

(Ladbroke Grove, 1968)

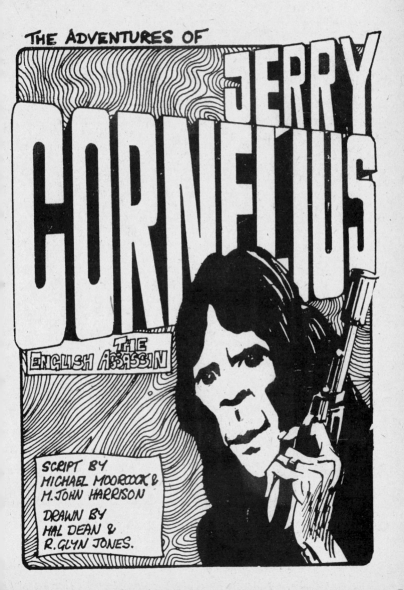

THE ADVENTURES OF JERRY CORNELIUS

THE ENGLISH ASSASSIN

SCRIPT BY
MICHAEL MOORCOCK &
M. JOHN HARRISON

DRAWN BY
HAL DEAN &
R. GLYN JONES.

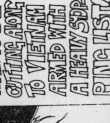

NUMBER ONE ON THE LIST ~GOODBYE MONDAY CLUB. TIME TO BE CUTTING ALONG TO VIETNAM ARMED WITH A HEAVY SPRING LIST!

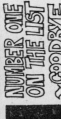

THE MONDAY CLUB !!!

ALL THE FOURS!!, OFFIZIERKORPS!!

SPLENDID, OH SPLENDID!

LEAVE THE HARDWARE WITH ME, PRETTY BOY. GET YOUR CARDS AT THE NEXT COUNTER.

FULL HOUSE !!!

YOU BUY FEELTHY PICTURES?

WHERE'S THE PINEAPPLE, CATHERINE?

GET THAT FRUIT PEELED!

BUT..

MISS BRUNNER!

GOD! SUSPENDERS! JERRY, BABY... YOU'RE ALL HUNG UP! IT'LL BE FRENCH KNICKERS NEXT!

NNNNNG.!!

JERRY IS TRAPPED ON MISS BRUNNERS LOGIC ESCALATOR. IT LOOKS AS IF HIS ONLY HOPE IS ANOTHER COP OUT..

SQUATTERS, EH?—AND COOKED UP GOOD!! THESE PLACES WEREN'T BUILT TO LAST.

WHITE CITY SHELTER
GOVT. PERSONNEL ONLY

SGT GLOGAUER IS WORRIED....

THIS ISN'T GOING THE WAY IT SHOULD. AND ALVAREZ ON THE OFF-SHIFT TOO.. THAT BLOODY ASSASSIN'LL HAVE TO GET HIS FINGERS OUT AND FIX THINGS SOON...

Meanwhile, back at the Time Centre...

ALL RIGHT, MISS B— HAVE IT YOUR OWN WAY...

"HAW! HAW! HAW! HOW'S THIS FOR A REALITY SYNDROME, MR. CORNELIUS?"

"YAHOOOO! THEIR WHOLE STRUCTURE'S COLLAPSING. IN A MOMENT THEY'LL BE OURS-FOR EVER!"

IT LOOKED HOPELESS, BUT JUST THEN—

"FRANK! THANK GOD...."

"IF YOU SAY SO. THERE'S ONLY ONE WAY OUT OF THIS-WE GOTTA TRY 'N' MAKE IT BACK TO CONDITION OR...."

OLD COLONEL CORNELIUS HAD JOSTLED THE LAMBDA JUST RIGHT IT SEEMED. SOON JERRY JOINED SISTER CATHY IN FRANCE & THE FAKE LeCORBUSIER CHATEAU — A PAUSE IN THE CONFLICT....

CATHY WAS IN AN UNUSUALLY INTROSPECTIVE MOOD. FOR GOOD REASON....

Peace on Earth

The *Trans-Galactos* came to a dead stop half a light year from the G-star. Within, its two occupants debated.

They were human, in the sense that they were the descendants of what had been human two million years ago and they still retained the bipedal, bimanual form. But they were lean and tall, with elongated faces, unhappy eyes and high brows which slanted sharply back. Their lank hair hung flaxen below their shoulders.

Most important, they were immortal.

At the moment, they were both feeling very uncertain of themselves. Fra-Thala held the Book in his hand as if it were a measure of reassurance. Bulik stared miserably at the G-star, Sol.

"We've got to try," Fra-Thala said. "We've got to. We can't let anything go by without trying."

"Try what? We don't even know what to look for."

"At least we can land and—look. Just look. It might be there—whatever it is."

Bulik continued to gaze at the star. He did not move.

"Go on," Fra-Thala told him. "Why don't you engage the

ship's drive? It's the third planet."

"I don't know," Bulik said slowly, almost whispering. "I think—I'm *scared*."

They were both silent for several seconds. They stared with strange fascination at Sol, a matter-of-fact, insignificant sun. Then Fra-Thala blanked out the viewport and the spell was lessened. The comforting walls of the ship were all about them.

"So you feel it too," he said.

"Fear?"

"Yes." Bulik's loosely jointed form paced the room. "But why?" he demanded. "We weren't afraid when we looked for it on Stulek Bal. We weren't afraid when someone told us it was in the Lesser Magellanic, or when we asked the Iddians for it. Why are we afraid now?"

Fra-Thala held up the black-bound Book. "Perhaps because this says Earth is where it really is."

"Why should that scare us?"

The other shrugged.

After a while, Bulik reluctantly made some computations. He looked again at Sol. Then he engaged the drive and the *Trans-Galactos* flashed to the region of the outermost planet, converted to interplanetary drive, and moved more slowly towards the Earth. Soon the ship was flooded with sunlight, which became gentle and diffused as they sank into the atmosphere of the third world, settling on to a vast arid plain.

The two men studied the landscape through the viewports. For five hundred years they had searched the galaxy until they had become gaunt with obsession. They had taken to gazing around them in a haunted way, as if the desperation of their quest had driven them into a misery and despair from which no force in the universe could rescue them.

And they were quite alone in their search. The *Trans-Galactos* was probably the only interstellar ship in the galaxy; they had built it themselves from ancient specifications. The rest of humanity lived placidly, aimlessly and immortally deep within the atmospheres of the settled planets. They had lost all meaning to life.

It was a meaning to life that Bulik and Fra-Thala sought. On the other side of the galaxy they had acquired the Book, written long ago by one of the greatest of all men, Aber Juillard, and real hope had for the first time presented itself. They did not know how long ago the book had been written, for it was made from imperishable material, but they knew it was about as old as the oldest man living, for among his other accomplishments, Juillard had also given mankind immortality. It had taken many years of research to discover that he had refused the gift himself and was no longer available.

Juillard had also foreseen that one day men would lose something from their lives, and had written of it in the Book. He had not stated exactly what it would be, and the passages referring to it were obscure, but it would seem to be something of immeasurable value. Fra-Thala had become filled with excitement when he read the sentence: "Those who wish to regain that precious thing that mankind loses should visit the planet Earth, the birthplace of the species, and there they shall find it."

Now he stared at the endless plain and felt hope sink again. He saw soft yellow dust strewn from here to the horizon, seeped in light from the low sun. The scene had such a delicate beauty as made him think of the meadows of his native world. Meadows of dust...

But nowhere was there any clue that might lead them to the unnamed object of their search.

A deep, moaning sigh escaped from Bulik. "It's no use!" he cried. "What is there here? Nothing. It's a dead world. Nothing lives. Nothing." He took the Book from his companion and read once again from the place they had marked. "This tells us nothing. He doesn't even mention anything specific. Perhaps it doesn't mean anything specific. Perhaps he was just being poetic."

"Even we can't say what we're looking for," Fra-Thala pointed out. "All we have is this terrible feeling inside us; this feeling of something missing. The passage in the book seems to be the same sort of thing."

He turned away from the viewport. The only label he could give it, he thought, was a desire for peace. Peace of mind, peace from the constant biting knowledge of something *gone*. There were centuries of life behind him: ahead was an eternity of trash, meaningless acts, futile existence.

Unless he could find this peace, this value that had vanished from the human mind.

"Well," he said, "let's look."

"Look? Where?" Bulik gestured to the waste outside the ship. "You can see everything from here."

"The Book—"

"The Book!" Bulik had lost all faith. He prowled the room, head bent, his cloak falling limply about him. "We've done what the Book said. We have come to Earth. And where are we? What have we found? Nothing. Juillard was being fanciful, I tell you!"

"No. He was too great for that. He had the finest understanding of human mentality of any creature before or since—he produced immortality, remember, on a purely mental level by adjusting the cortical control of physiological processes. I can't believe that he would write those words without good reason."

He glanced again at the viewport. "You're right, there's nothing in this desert. But the Earth's a fair-sized planet and it was well populated once. Let's move over the horizon until we find something."

Bulik frowned, then moved to the control panel.

After a few moments the ship lifted twenty feet from the surface and travelled in the direction of the sun. As an afterthought he activated the detector to show the presence of refined metals.

This last action paid off. They travelled about a hundred miles without any change in the ochre desert before the indicator flashed. Bulik put the ship into a slow circle, seeking the object of response.

It was a thick, flat cylindrical building, standing solidly on the desert floor and throwing off the cold light of afternoon as it must have done for countless thousands of years: it was so long since there had been living things on Sol's third planet that the air itself had become unbreathable.

"It could be anything," Bulik said, "but let's get out there and see. I hope there's a way in."

There was. Fra-Thala walked nearly the full circumference, the boots of his light-weight atmosphere suit scuffing up dust, before he found it; a simple sliding door, its bearings cunningly protected against abrasion and time. The building gave the impression of having been built to endure.

When they got inside and switched on their torches, Bulik snorted with disappointment. "Why, it's just a bookvault. I've seen them a hundred times."

They wandered around for several minutes, without real interest. It was common practice for a community to leave samples and records of its culture when it abandoned a region and there was no reason to suppose there was anything special about this one, or about the society it represented.

Or was there? Fra-Thala awoke to the situation with a start. Since Earth was the original planet, the vault might contain traces of the most primeval periods, back before spaceflight. That in itself was rather unremarkable, but the Book...

With slightly more alertness, he took up a few of the volumes from their cases. He was pleased to find that although some of the languages and symbolisms were very ancient he was acquainted with most of them. An immortal has time to learn most things sooner or later. But after a little study his interest waned again. There was nothing he would not have expected, or that he might not have encountered on a thous- and worlds.

Bulik was ambling moodily throughout the extent of the vault. Now he came up to Fra-Thala to see what he was doing. "Do you think—do you think it *might* be here after all? Should we examine every one of these books, because the secret of it might be written here somewhere?" He seemed pathetically dismayed.

"No, I don't think so. Juillard wouldn't be so tedious, I'm sure of that. This is just an ordinary culture vault."

Bulik considered, nodded and looked relieved. "I suppose you're right. Let's get out of here. It makes me feel irritable. I could do with some sleep."

Fra-Thala remembered that he also had not slept for a considerable time. Carelessly replacing the books in their cases he followed his companion, stumbling towards the block of pale-gold light that came from the open door.

Outside, he found that he had forgotten to replace one book. Mildly curious, he looked at the obsolescent script imprinted on the cover: *The Thousand and One Nights*. He flicked through it, stopped at a page and read:

"... and he and the King and his father-in-law and their family resided in the most happy state and in the practice of good deeds, until they were visited by the terminator of delights, and the separator of companions."

He stared at the sentence blankly for a short time, and shuddered. Life, to an immortal, was most carefully guarded, and the loss of it was looked on with the greatest horror. The very suggestion of death would make a man look frantically about him for a source of danger.

Letting the book drop from his hand into the dust, he trudged wearily towards the *Trans-Galactos*.

A few hours later, Fra-Thala awoke to the realization that uneasiness had not left him since they had made the stop far beyond Pluto. It had stayed with him through the sleeping period, producing restless dreams.

He had dreamed that he was back on his home world before he had met Bulik and their twin frustrations had flared into life on contact. In the dream, it was as if he could see millions of years ahead of time. The people of the town where he was born had stared at him with stupefied eyes, stultified, gaping, grey with decay because they had lived for so long without the thing that would make them completely human. On waking he felt no horror but lay with his eyes closed, going over the details of the nightmare and letting his detached intellect extract the full sense from it. It would not take millions of years, he thought; it would only take thousands. It might have begun already.

It might happen to him, and to Bulik, unless they found the answer in time. He tried to examine his own mind, to find out what it was that was worrying him about this planet; but the question receded further and further from him as he approached it.

He rose from the sleeping couch, rinsed his face with ice-cold water and combed out his long hair where he had been lying on it. Usually when he woke he ate, but now food seemed like sacrilege to him. Night had come and gone, and it was early morning. He looked at the small G-star which was pouring its perpetual energy over the landscape.

Fra-Thala shook his head. The terrible idea came to him that perhaps humanity was already too far gone to retrieve the precious item it had lost, like a corpse already on the road to decomposition. Perhaps he and Bulik would wander for centuries about the galaxy, never achieving their purpose, until the purpose became submerged in an inertia of mindless meandering.

With that thought in his head he seated himself at the control panels, his glazed eyes falling automatically on the multitude of meters. He blinked apathetically—then stood, suddenly vitalized with intelligence.

"Bulik! Here!"

Bulik continued to sleep. Impatiently he strode over to the couch and shook him roughly awake, dragged him over to the panels. Bulik shielded his eyes as the sharp sunlight fell on them.

"Look!" Fra-Thala said, pointing. "The detector shows another energy converter on the planet. It must be another ship!"

Adjusting his eyes to the light, Bulik read the meter. There could be no mistake: nothing had the same composition of materials as an energy converter. "From the look of it," he stated, "the converter has ceased functioning as an energy source. Probably an abandoned ship, or a derelict. It must have been here all the time and we never thought to check."

"Shall we go and see it?"

Bulik shrugged. "If you like. I don't suppose there'll be much to learn."

He moved the *Trans-Galactos* a few miles for a triangulation fix and located the converter at a place somewhere around what was currently midday. As he geared the drive for the transplanetary hop, the yellow waste swayed beneath them and Sol rose swiftly into the sky. But the living quarters of the ship, with their own independent gravitation, were a closed system: it was as if the Earth moved and the room stayed still. Not even the sound of the air rushing over the exterior surface penetrated its calm. It might have been a staid dwelling on some garden world.

The sight of the other ship, when they found it, verified the opinion that it had lain motionless for a considerable time. Dust, blown by vagrant thin winds, had piled up on one side of it: the entire length of the vessel had bellied a few feet into the desert.

They went outside to inspect the ship, and Fra-Thala ran his gloved hand along the smooth metal. It was impossible to tell by appearance whether it had been built ten years ago or ten thousand, since the materials were of the permanent kind produced by molecular impaction: its position, however, and the fact that its power source had died, suggested an age of several millennia.

Bulik tried to open the airlock. It did not respond. "As I thought," he said. "The ship's completely without power." As he applied the emergency power pack to the external leads, the lock door slid aside with a whine, and they were able to step inside a vessel patterned largely after their own. Fra-Thala began to feel a kinship with the owners, for the chances were that they came from his section of the galaxy.

They opened the door to the living quarters. Yellow light streamed through dusty viewports into a room in perfect condition, and without trace of an occupant.

Several minutes still elspased before Fra-Thala reached the quite obvious conclusion that this ship had landed long after the Earth's population had vanished, and then the owner had vanished also. The realization came as a shock. "Bulik!" Fra-Thala fought against a great sense of panic. "Bulik! What happened to the man?"

For a moment Bulik was unable to answer. His face was colourless. "There couldn't have been...*danger*."

"But where *is* he?"

Bulik shook his head.

Fra-Thala felt his nagging undercurrent of fear mount to a momentary climax of desperation. It was like being told that the spacecraft in which he was travelling was caught in a magnetic storm which would not fail to sweep it into a white-hot star. He peered about him for some clue.

He found one thing. A book, bound in black. A copy of Juillard's Book.

Amazed he snatched it up. It was identical to his own, the same edition. "So there are others," he murmured. "Others with the same yearning. They obtained the Book—and they too followed its instructions."

"Were others," corrected Bulik. "They're not here any more."

"But what happened? Perhaps they found it." Like a dynamo rising to its full speed he suddenly became full of excitement. "Perhaps they found what they wanted—the secret of life!"

"Then why did they desert the ship?"

He fingered the imperishable volume, not knowing the answer. Eventually he said: "Who knows what the secret of life brings? Perhaps they no longer needed the ship."

His companion was not impressed. "That sounds rather fanciful. A more prosaic theory would suit me better."

Fra-Thala was prepared to admit that he was allowing his imagination free play. The bewilderment of their discoveries had released him into uninhibited dreams: for never before had they met companions in their search, apart from the sentiments expressed by the long-dead Aber Juillard.

And never before, in mankind's thinly-spread but super-cautious society, had they heard of men who disappeared without a trace. An immortal life was far too precious a thing to take chances with.

"Listen," he urged, "there's a lead here—there's something to learn. There must be—the circumstances are too unusual. We must follow it up!"

"How?" Bulik had been searching the chamber for further information. He found none, except that there were two sleeping couches, indicating that the expedition consisted of a corresponding number. "This ship was abandoned ages ago."

Fra-Thala shook his head. "You can always manage to dampen my enthusiasm, Bulik."

A few minutes later they gave up and decided to go back to their own vessel. Fra-Thala still retained a feeling of unrest: and as they crossed the few yards between ships he lifted his head and surveyed the land. Through the thin material of his atmosphere suit he felt an insubstantial cold wind press against him, a wind that had swept the full length of the plain, down from those hills in the distance, and perhaps halfway across the face of the planet. Something in him stirred.

"You know," he said, "we haven't really carried out Juillard's instructions. Not yet."

"What do you mean?"

"Juillard said to go to Earth. Well, we've landed here,

that's all. We've spent about twenty minutes in all outside our ship, and the rest of the time we've cowered inside it. We should get to know what it feels like to be on Earth, walk about on the ground, explore by foot.''

He could see Bulik hesitating. ''All right,'' the man admitted at last, ''perhaps you've got something. Perhaps that is what he meant. Let's do it.''

For both of them the act took a tremendous effort of will. Drawing strength from one another, they set out towards the hills which undulated on the horizon. Fra-Thala felt strangely light-headed and he sensed that his companion did too. After half a mile he turned to look back at the two starships, and his fear mounted again, without reason, like an animal bolting from a sudden noise. Yet he did not question what he hoped to find in the hills: he had a childlike compulsion to obey Juillard, and this was how he thought it should be done. Nervously they advanced together over the dead, brightly shining expanse.

By mid-afternoon they had gained the hills. There was not much difference: the ground still consisted of yellow dust lain on solid bedrock, but in places the stone was revealed and glittered as if showing its strength. Fra-Thala walked away up a gently rising slope and swivelled his eyes about. His attention was easily caught by the one item of interest.

His lungs snatched air in nausea and shock some seconds before the logical part of his mind recognized the object. It was the remains of a skeleton.

He ran over to it, frantically motioning Bulik to follow. ''The poor fellow! What can have happened? He—he *died*.''

He uttered the word in a tone of utter horror. He had never seen a deceased human before.

The man's atmosphere suit was lying some yards away. For some reason which Fra-Thala could not possibly guess at, he had seen fit to crawl out of it before dying—indeed, he could hardly have hoped to survive the act. Bulik inspected the suit: the perishable components had disintegrated, and the rest couldn't tell him much. ''Well,'' he said, ''now we know why the ship's empty.''

Fra-Thala pointed out slowly: ''Our ship's empty, now.''

In an instant he became terribly afraid. ''Let's get back,'' he urged. ''Quick. Now!''

Bulik did not need to voice his agreement. Striding rapidly, they fled in the direction of the *Trans-Galactos*. For no particular reason Fra-Thala glanced at his airmeter. He froze.

"Bulik... how's your air?"

His companion checked his own supply, and moaned in fright. "Nearly gone!"

"Mine, too..." Incredulously, he glared at the meter. He couldn't begin to understand. "How could we have been so careless! I never heard of anyone being so stupid..."

His voice trailed off, paralysed by the magnitude of the disaster. He thought of running for it, but simultaneously there came the realization that they just would not reach the ship in time.

He squatted down in the dust, shaking his head. He could not believe that their forgetting to renew the air supply was pure accident; men didn't make mistakes like that any more than they forgot to breathe. Men never took chances on their lives.

Yet he was to die. Soon.

His brain refused to carry the meditation any further. Alarmed that he could accept the idea of death, he tried to shake himself into action, made a tremendous effort to grasp the situation entirely...

And then he knew why he was going to die.

Looking up, he saw that Bulik had found the answer as well. Wordlessly they communicated their twin discoveries.

What was it that in primeval times had given form and significance to a human being's existence? A thing is worthwhile only because of the possibility of its removal: the factor was death. Fra-Thala remembered the story he had taken from the book-vault, and realized that the King and his family could not have lived happily had they been immortal.

"Bulik," he said in surprise, "so that was why we were afraid. Death is what we fear most of all—and death is what we were seeking. Juillard knew of the consequences of never-ending life. So he left a way out for those who are sensitive enough to desire it. That's why we were careless about our air supply: it was a subconscious suggestion implanted along with the immortality equations."

The other nodded. Then they both hunched silently on the

ground, breathing the oxygen remaining in their packs. Fra-Thala died shortly afterwards, but the intervening few seconds of his life were charged with meaning.

(Chelsea, 1958,
with Barrington Bayley)

The Lovebeast

THEY MUST LET ME IN—*I can love them. They must let me in!*

He is drifting, invisible, in the upper atmosphere and there is a longing in him. He has been there, and on the surface, for many centuries now—knowing what he needs but not quite strong enough to do anything to achieve it. He requires only an opportunity but it has never come. Not once in all those years has the world, as a whole, given him his opportunity. He doesn't know whence he came nor how he arrived on this planet. He cannot leave—he is in love.

He is a lonely beast, and his loneliness is heightened by his intelligence, which is very great.

Let me love you—let me.

For his love is selfless and he will not force it upon the world. His agony is terrible and it is true that in a hundred years or so he will die.

There is not much more time.

Curtis walked slowly down the middle of the village street, his blood tingling.

He entered Adam Turner's cluttered general store and

listened to the jangling music until Turner came into the front of the shop. The old man switched off the radio and said: "You've heard the latest report too, eh, Charlie?"

Curtis nodded. "Is it really the end of the human race, Adam? The papers said it would be—some of *us* said it would be. But I don't think I ever believed it."

"Do you believe it now, Charlie?"

"Yes."

The tone of the newspapers had been too subdued—the voice of the news announcer had been grim and filled with fear. Charles Curtis believed it now. Curtis, the frustrated artist who painted signs for a living, had been able to conceive the end of humanity as something possible, much as he dreaded the idea. But radioactive fall-out would not be the cause, he had told himself—that was a bogey exploited by sensation-seeking newspapers and people who wanted to stop the manufacture of nuclear bombs.

Two years before, the East had set off three huge nuclear explosions in outer space and the West had responded with four even bigger ones. And so the ridiculous game of Who's-got-the-most-Power? continued until the upper atmosphere had become choked with radiation. The representatives of nations were worried but they wavered. One Premier had been pressured by his military chiefs to detonate just one more bomb—so others followed suit. And now the radiation was everywhere. People were dying all over the world—dying horribly. Populations were in a state of despair and agony.

The Sunday after the news had been released, Curtis had gone to church as usual, striving to recapture some of the faith that had been flagging in him gradually for the last five years. But he had not been successful. As far as Curtis was concerned, God had abandoned the Earth to its self-chosen fate.

"But is it *fair*, Adam?" he said. "Is it fair? A few men in positions of power instruct their technicians and scientists to construct multi-megaton bombs so that they can demonstrate just how much personal power they held in their hands. They claim that they represent the peoples of their respective nations. Some of these people may even believe this in their hearts—they may be honest men. Yet they are only succeeding in killing us all—or most of us. Is there any chance, I wonder, of a few of us surviving?"

"There's nowhere to escape—nowhere in the world." Adam Turner spoke dully. He was thinking of his long-dead wife and of his married daughter living in London. He was glad that his wife was dead.

"No chance, you think?" Curtis's eyes were wet.

"Who knows? A few may live—some may adapt. What's it called...?"

"Mutate," supplied Curtis. "But they won't really be human, will they? I mean, not like us. I wonder if it matters..."

The door of the shop opened as Mrs. Vaughan came in. The bell didn't ring until after the door had closed again. The girl, recently married to a young farm worker, was buxom and pale. The shopping bag which had always been with her when she left her house was not on her arm.

"Have we got it?" Her voice was thick, almost hysterical. "Have we got it, Mr Turner—Mr Curtis. *Have we?*"

"Christ!" Curtis turned away and leant both hands on the shop counter. Yes, they all had it. He could feel it in his bones —in his blood, in his flesh and his brain. In his soul, perhaps? It was there. Radiation sickness—the disease one never belie-ved was real.

"Can't we get injections or something? He didn't say on the radio. Can't they stop it?"

"*No!*" Curtis wheeled around and confronted the fright-ened girl. "No! No, Mrs Vaughan, there's nothing they can» do. We're all going to die!"

"Shut up, Charlie!" Turner shouted. "Shut up, you idiot!"

Curtis couldn't stop. He knew he shouldn't be reacting this way—but he simply couldn't stop: "There's nothing any more, Adam—nothing to look forward to. No hope, no chance. No injections or safety precautions—no shelters. Nothing, Adam—absolutely nothing in the Universe that can save us. Do you realize that? In the whole of infinity there is nothing that can stop this. We are all going to suffer death—and we are not even going to die decently. We're going to rot away— our bones are going to crumble and the flesh fall away from them. The planet is stricken with the plague of man's foolish-ness and cowardice.

"Adam—we can't even die bravely—fighting..."

Curtis was dazed. Mrs Vaughan, terrified, shocked by his

words, fled sobbing from the shop. Curtis shrugged and started to follow her out.

Turner said: "You bloody fool. And you talk of cowardice."

But Curtis wasn't afraid. Curtis was hurt and bewildered. More so than ever, now, he felt the wisdom of the Sanskrit *sultras*. Everything seemed illusory—a bad dream. Was it worth clinging to reality, still? Could he find comfort in believing that what was happening now didn't matter—that it was the ordained and irrevocable *karma* of the world to die in this way?

He began to walk towards the pub.

There was that line of Eliot's which everyone quoted when the poet's name was mentioned—the line from *The Hollow Men: This is the way the world ends—this is the way the world ends—not with a bang, but a whimper...* Curtis almost laughed. How precisely the poet had described the present situation. And now he remembered that line of Donne's, too— a line also pertinent to his present predicament: *Any man's death diminishes me—for I am involved in humanity...*

"Any man's death dimishes me." Curtis had the same feeling. He knew, deep within him, what Donne meant. Curtis, too, sensed his own involvement. He felt as if he were part of some great being—a being which had possessed infinite potential but was now slowly dying, cell by cell. All over the world, the cells were crumbling and the great being which, in recent years, had come more and more to represent God to Curtis, was dying. And there was no other world, no after-life for a planet and its population, its mountains and its buildings and its forests. They were all the same thing and the whole set-up was destined to die and could never exist again in that form—the form which Curtis loved so much.

As the men of the world died in hopeless terror and slow agony, Curtis felt himself diminishing, being destroyed piece by piece—spiritually and physically. For in his own body, as in the body of the world, the sickness was intruding further—eating into him, rotting him, killing him body and soul.

The King's Head was open—it had not closed for long in the past two days—and Curtis entered its cool, dark confines, surprised to see that only a couple of the old men were sitting at the bar with their dogs lying beside them.

"'Morning, Peter—'morning Edward," he said. The old

men nodded and smiled. "Where is everybody, Edward?"

"Dunno, Mister Curtis. Some's gone to church. Some's at home—not many's workin' today." Edward Cray threw some money on the bar, the coins clattering loudly. He shouted: "Pint of best, Henry!" He turned enquiringly to Curtis. "That's what you'll have, eh, Mister Curtis?"

"Thanks, Edward—but you can't afford it on your pension, I'll get it."

Cray smiled a thin, tired, old man's smile. "Don't think I'll have to worry, Mister Curtis. I always promised myself I'd buy you one back some day—and I can do it now, can't I? I'm not so sure there'll be anyone to pay out next week's pension—nor whether there'll be anyone to collect it, either..."

Curtis thanked Cray as Henry, the landlord, put the brimming glass mug on the bar. He threw the money in the till, not even bothering to ring it up. He grinned at Curtis. But couldn't disguise the fear behind his eyes. "Don't know why I bother to take money, Mr. Curtis. But it's habit, you know—and for me to give the beer away would be an empty sort of generosity, wouldn't it?"

"I suppose so," Curtis agreed.

The beer, he expected, was radioactive, too. Why, then, was he pouring it down his throat? Didn't taste any different...

He hoped Edward hadn't been hurt by Henry's talk of empty generosity. Curtis accepted the drink in the spirit the old man had offered it. He thanked Cray and offered to buy a fresh round. The two men nodded approval.

Peter Baker bent down with difficulty and scratched his black spaniel behind the ears. "I hope she goes first," he muttered. "She'd pine without me."

Edward chuckled: "I'm an evil old man," he said. "My Janet always told me that. I'm near me time, anyway—but I get a funny sort of satisfaction, you might say, from knowing that all them others is going too. I won't be lonely, will I, Mr. Curtis?"

"No, Edward," Curtis said.

He drank his beer as quickly as he could.

"I'm off home now," he told them. "See you this evening, perhaps."

"Aye," Cray chuckled. "Maybe, Mr. Curtis—maybe..."

Trembling, Curtis left the pub and walked the hundred

yards to his cottage, passing the houses where people sat—wondering and waiting. He unlatched the door of the cottage and went straight up the uncarpeted stairs.

Here, the single room of the upper storey had been converted by Curtis into a studio. His paintings were heaped everywhere, together with lettered signs and rough drawings. He kicked at the pile of finished signs, sending them scattering.

Did this impending horror help, he asked himself, when it came to painting? Could he create something worth while at last—as he died? A canvas was ready, prepared, on the easel. His brushes were on the table, with his palette and his colours. He inhaled the smell of linseed oil—the smell he loved. Could he paint a picture which would symbolize everything he felt—everything the world was feeling? He knew he could try and that his effort would come close to doing what he wanted to express. In the dark corner of the studio, hardly visible in the shadow, a camp bed had been erected. This was where he slept sometimes, when he had been working late. He couldn't bring himself to pick up the brushes, to mix his colours.

Instead, he walked towards the bed and lowered himself wearily on to it. He knew that his energy was failing—that all his vitality was being consumed by his body to resist the sickness in his bloodstream—to fight, though hopelessly. Well, at least I am fighting, he thought, Unconsciously, perhaps—but fighting, nonetheless.

He lay back with his hands folded on his chest.

Any man's death diminishes me...

If only there were something. Miracles were needed. Big miracles. There was no hope—nowhere in the Universe was there a spark of hope. If only there were...

He was beginning to go to sleep. Vague memories were combining with his wandering imagination so that he heard fragments of conversation that had never been, saw faces that were half-familiar, became aware of situations which he had never known before. Was this, perhaps, his last sleep...?

But something else was pervading his confused half-dream. A peculiar something—a feeling of—desperate warmth... Was this death? No...

Let me in. Let me love you—let me love...

Curtis did not dare break his tenuous, delicate link with... Himself? His subconscious? No, it was more than the usual

Michael Moorcock

dream-before-sleeping fantasy. This was something outside—
something new.

Where are you? he asked silently. *What do you want?*

Then it burst through, filling all of him. His mind, his brain,
his body was full of warmth—no longer desperate. Now it was
joyous, grateful...

*In all the days I have lived, I have begged you to be loved.
For my sake, let me love you.*

Where are you? Curtis was sitting up on the shaking bed.
He had an impression, not only of love but of great intelligence. And the words... They were not actually from the
source. Certainly the feeling was expressed in the words, but
—*they were his own words!* The words he had used once in an
old poem.

"Who are you?" he said aloud now.

Lovebeast loves world...

"What? Where are you from?"

Know not. My love is here, if you desire it...

It was becoming almost too much for Curtis's tired brain.
Was he suffering from hallucinations induced by the sickness
in him? Could he really believe this?

*Please don't fear—please don't question. I can love you—
love you all...*

"But—how? What should we do to gain your love? When
did you come? Did you hear of our plight?"

*A million years I have been in love with you, but you have
never given me the opportunity I needed to show you my love.
Where is the rest of you? I can love it all—all of you...*

Curtis felt frantic, but he was also filled with hoy—fresh
hope.

"We must all open ourselves to your love—is that it? Every
one of us must allow himself to be loved."

*Yes! Yes! Communicate this to the rest of you. Let me love
you—there is so little time left... For centuries, hundreds of
centuries, I have wanted to love you and now, in the last few
moments of my old age, I may yet be able to...*

Curtis rushed for his station wagon, knowing that it would
take at least three hours to reach the capital. But there was the
means he needed to broadcast his message of hope to a world
that had begun to accept the prospect of death with a hopeless,

apathetic fatalism.

He was at last admitted to an office. A tired man sitting behind a desk said: "You're not the only one who wants to use our transmitters, Mr. Curtis. We've had dozens of applications, you know."

Curtis said levelly: "I appreciate that you must have. But I think my message may be instrumental in saving the world. You must admit that anything is worth trying."

Please let me love you... The Lovebeast was still with him, its messages weirdly pathetic for one of its powers and intelligence. The world must accept its love, Curtis thought, as he reasoned with the man behind the desk. He was sure that if it did, then the world would be saved.

The official sighed: "Very well, Mr. Curtis. We'll announce your broadcast on all networks. The rest is up to you. I don't expect you to be successful, any more than all the other cranks we've allowed to broadcast. But you seem a trifle more reasonable and it's worth the chance. What is it you want to say exactly?"

Curtis was cautious, aware of the reception he would receive if he mentioned the Lovebeast beforehand.

"Just listen," he said. "Listen when I make my broadcast."

I am ready to love you—as ready as I have been in a million years. Please—please—do not disappoint me now...

He waited impatiently for the people to make their announcement. Then he was escorted to a studio and had to wait patiently once more while networks were cleared. Then he was ready—ready to broadcast his message of hope to the world.

He stuttered his first words, conscious that his voice was going out to all people, translated into many different tongues.

"There... there is hope." He had to force himself to speak clearly and calmly. "Somewhere about the Earth there is a... being... an unhuman entity which has come from a different galaxy—perhaps a different dimension—and it can help us.

"It can help us." Curtis spoke confidently now. "Believe that. It is our only chance and we must take it. This entity can only help us if we allow it to. *If we let it into ourselves.* All we need to do is relax and let this being see that we are ready to receive its love—and its help.

"We have nothing to lose.

"I know you may think I sound like a madman—that many

of you will disbelieve what I have told you. But I ask you all—every man, woman and child on the Globe—to test the truth of my words…'' He glanced at the big studio clock. ''At twenty-four-hundred hours, GMT, be ready—open your hearts and minds to receive this entity's love. Remember, it is our chance for survival—our chance to correct the ghastly mistake we have made—our chance to live and make a better world. *Let him love you.''*

There was nothing more for Curtis to say. He hoped he had been coherent enough—that all the nations of Earth had given him a chance to be heard. There were three hours still to go.

''We'll keep playing the recording,'' a technician said. The man was almost smiling. ''I hope to God you've got something —and I think you have.''

Curtis nodded to him: ''I hope everybody thinks so,'' he said softly.

He had lost a great deal of faith in the human race during recent weeks and he was not sure, even now, because of their stupid pride, that they would accept this final chance. He hoped that they would—but how could he be certain? He could only wait—with the Beast for company.

Are you ready? Are you ready? love…

Not yet, he said, as he drove wildly home. *Not yet…*

When? There was longing and pain in the word.

Soon. There was a trace of uncertainty in his answer. *Soon.*

He is drifting closer to Earth, together with the poisoning radiation of which he is unaware—the radiation which has, ironically, given him the opportunity he had sought for so long. His vast, amorphous being encircles the world—waiting impatiently, expectantly—even humbly.

Soon. Soon I will love you all..

He will receive nothing from those he wishes to love. He desires nothing save the vessels for the huge love within him and around him. He can give. This is his purpose. To give. To give. To bestow love.

The Lovebeast drifts closer and closer.

Soon—soon.

Curtis scrambled from the station wagon and burst into Turner's still-open shop. Adam Turner, his friend, was waiting for him calmly.

"Well," he said, "we all heard your broadcast. I don't know what this is, Charlie, but I hope you're right. How do you know about this—this Beast of Love—whatever it is? How did you contact it?"

"I don't know," Curtis replied. "But I don't think that I've been the first individual to make contact with its 'aura', anyway. Perhaps I've been the first to communicate with it, recognize it for what it is—an alien entity from a different part of the Universe. Maybe people under great emotional and intellectual stress are good 'mediums' for contacting the Beast..."

There were only five minutes to go.

They went back into the living room behind the shop. They sat down.

Now but three minutes to go.

Adam was frowning.

Now—now. May I love you now?

Soon, Curtis told the Lovebeast. *Soon.*

Adam smiled: "You know, Charlie, I *do* sense something..."

...One minute.

Yes, you are ready—I think—almost...

This is their last chance, Curtis thought desperately. Their last chance. They *must* take it!

Yes!

And then the love came.

All over the world, those who still lived felt its warmth flowing into them. Men who had never been happy before became overjoyed. Men remembered times when, for no reason at all, they had been caught up in a happiness resembling this— when they had been filled with love for the world, for no reason, for no reason. And now they knew from where this spirit had emanated. Love—pure, selfless love, flowed through the world, bringing hope to the hopeless. Comfort— new life.

Upon all the lands of the Earth, in all the people of every nation, in cities and villages, the forests and in the mountains and upon the plains, wherever men were living, the joy came —bursting upwards from within them. It filled them.

Of course, some had paid no attention to Curtis's broadcast —others had not heard it. But the majority of cells in that great Earth Body had seized their chance, opening up the breech the Lovebeast had so long yearned for. And the small minority were caught up in its love before they realized it.

It was a quality of love that made the people feel humble before it even as they rejoiced—for it was a love of such tenderness, such humility, such sympathy...

Pure love—selfless love.

The Lovebeast gave at last. Gave of his great store which had been building up within him for a million years. Gave and gave and gave until those who received him—and there were still left many millions—felt they could absorb no more of this wondrous joy. But they could.

And they did, as the Lovebeast lavished its love, generously and with tenderness.

And now the cry came from the minds of those millions united by the love of the Beast, sensing, at last, that they were all of the same flesh, all part of the same body. They were now unified in love—the same thing—involved—blended with one another. The cry came from the Earth:

YOU WHO LOVE US—SAVE US NOW FROM DESTRUCTION.

The Lovebeast fed its love to the object of its love. At first it was oblivious of the cry, not sensing it.

The world was sure of salvation. It looked forward to a new, brilliant phase in its history—a return to Grace...

OH, LOVEBEAST—SAVE US NOW...

The Lovebeast heard the words at last—and finally it understood them. But it was bewildered.

Save you? Save you—my love?

The Lovebeast was puzzled. What could this mean? A peculiar development. What was wrong?

He tried to grasp at the full significance of the words, but something stopped him. He couldn't quite reach them. The concept was—alien.

Save you? I cannot interfere. I love you. I love you, too much ...I cannot save you—I can love you—this is my purpose—to love you. Love you—you—love—love—love.

- Norbury, 1957

Three

The Real Life Mr Newman

(Adventures of the Dead Astronaut)

THE LONDON FOG was lifting. In Charing Cross Gardens the black skeletons of trees became visible and Newman could just see the shadowy buildings beyond them. As the fog dispersed he got up from the bench, not welcoming the change in the weather.

He seemed to be the only person about.

London was still silent as he swung his huge body, swaddled in its thick, tan overcoat, towards the Embankment, plodded through the gates of the gardens and out into the main road. He ran across the road, noticing the stationary bus and wondering briefly why the passengers sat so still. He leaned on the Embankment wall, peering down into the river.

For a moment the river, too, seemed petrified—but then he saw that he had been mistaken. It was moving, very sluggishly; alive with bobbing refuse, stained with oil. Turning his head to his right, Newman saw the ugly railway bridge with its rusted steel and peeling green paint, a suburb-bound train clanking across it. On his left was white Waterloo Bridge, marked by its orange lights, curving over the water like a graceful sea-beast. And across the river, marked only by the patches of light breaking through the fog, was the Festival Hall. Newman turned and leant against the wall, staring across the road at the entrance to Charing Cross Underground Station.

Newman had expected the fog to last much longer and was now disappointed. He was never afraid in the fog.

Near the Underground entrance a few vague shapes moved —grey figures who emerged from the fog and became black silhouettes in the light of the station foyer.

He crossed the road in a lumbering run, skipped hastily on to the pavement, a hooting taxi missing him narrowly, and rushed into the lobby. He paused, fumbling in his coat for change. He put his money into a ticket machine, took his ticket from the slot and walked slowly to the barrier. The attendant didn't seem to notice him as he went through.

He had gone past the barrier and was about to step on to the downward escalator when he paused and began to tremble. He could not calm the trembling. It became violent.

For a few seconds he fought to conquer his fear, but it was hopeless. He couldn't bring himself to take a single step towards the escalator. It was well lit; he could see to the bottom where a short tunnel led to the platform. The layout of the station was familiar to him. There was no danger. But he could go no further. He turned and stumbled back through the barrier, out of the station by its other entrance and up Villiers Street, still dark and silent, towards Trafalgar Square.

As the fog dispersed Newman's peace of mind evaporated. He now felt troubled, persecuted. He ran faster when he reached the Strand and turned towards Trafalgar Square. Then he stopped dead again at what he thought he saw.

Nelson's Column had grown to gigantic size. It seemed to fill the whole square with its grimy masonry, stretching above him into the remnants of the rising fog. He shut his eyes and rubbed them—for him, a normal habit. When he opened them again the column had grown even larger. He raced down the Strand away from it, colliding with several people as he ran.

Now the rest of the buildings began to increase in size. Even passers-by seemed larger. Vast walls of concrete towered higher and higher—no longer buildings, but sheer, cave-studded sides of immense black cliffs. He charged on through canyons that seemed to fold in upon him. Blurs of light—red, blue, green, orange—darted like fire-flies before his eyes. There were noises; distant roars and shrieks. There was the sensation of blows on his body, and everywhere the smell of iodine and almonds. Vibrating lines attacked his face and veered off as he raised his pale hands against them. His lungs were filled with a million tiny, stabbing icicles, his stomach was hollow, painful; his legs liquid, without bone or muscle.

The solid, thrumming note of a drum filled his skull—the sound of his maddened pulse as his heart sought to free itself from its cage of flesh and ribs. His breathing was a series of huge gasps—he could not get enough of the thin air. Booted feet ached, thighs and groin throbbed; hands waved on bruised arms—hands like peeled sticks waving in a high wind.

As a boy in England and later in Virginia, where his mother had gone with her American husband, Newman had admired trees more than anything else. He liked them green and golden and rustling in summer; he liked them stark and black and brittle in winter. He rarely broke a branch or stripped a twig of its bark or its leaves. He liked sometimes to climb them in summer, particularly when climbing helped him breathe in their sweetness and look down at a surging sea of foliage. But most of the time he had liked simply to walk among their trunks or lie in their shade, his back to the grass. He had resented it if he had been called away from the woods, where he would have drowned among trees if it had been possible.

"Alexander!" his mother used to call in her half-English accent. "Are you there?"

"Come on, Al!" The good-natured voice of his stepfather, slightly embarrassed by the authority over her child which marrying Alexander's mother had given him.

Usually Alexander would come when called. He was an obedient child. But sometimes he would hide, or creep deeper into the woods that went on without end at the back of the house. He had fancied sometimes that the house stood on the edge of civilisation—beyond it, endless forests without houses or human beings. He didn't need to populate this forest of his imagination; the forest was enough.

He had been a cheerful boy, lonely by choice. He had mixed well enough at school, sometimes playing with the neighbourhood children. He had been personable and clever, though he absorbed knowledge intuitively rather than consciously. Exams would release facts he didn't know he knew. He didn't object to following his stepfather into the Air Force when he left college—he had majored in physics—and he became an efficient, mildly-liked officer. He was one of the men selected to go up in a space capsule when the Space Project got under way.

Col. Alexander Newman, USAF, ran blindly through the transformed streets of a terrifying London. Since his flight was silent, he was cursed rather than restrained by the people he bumped into. He didn't look very different from a commuter late for his train. He ran down the Strand, past Aldwych, where cars braked as he crossed their paths, up Fleet Street until, exhausted, he stopped, drained of adrenalin. The aural and visual sensations diminished and disappeared. His physical sensations remained. His mouth was dry and he was wet with sweat.

He looked up at the *Daily Express* building. It had the appearance of a monstrous, Edwardian public lavatory and wash-house, covered in shiny tiles. He knew then that he was in Fleet Street. He hadn't come particularly far—but he couldn't remember how he had got here. Something like this had happened several times before, he thought. He looked at his watch. It had stopped. He pulled up his coat collar, wiping the sweat from his face. No-one seemed to be looking at him, so he decided that his behaviour hadn't been too abnormal. He hailed a taxi, climbed in and gave the address.

A towering, glowering, twisted London went past as the driver took him towards Notting Hill. Nothing looked man-made. Everything had the appearance of a strange, natural landscape—canyons and crags, grey and black, with dim lights gleaming here and there. Asymmetrical, it had an air of being as yet only partly formed, waiting for a shape that would be given it. The shape, Newman felt, would not be that of the London he knew.

The sense of menace increased as the taxi sped on and he controlled his urge to tell the driver to stop.

Above all, Newman thought, it was bleak; it was a waste-land. It had never been alive.

Yet there was life there—life in it, like the maggots in a corpse. Life in the tall, brooding cliffs, hollowed by a million burrows. Life full of misery and disease and hopeless repetit-ion of senseless actions. Life neurotic. Nothing could make it worse than it was, and only total destruction, perhaps, could improve it.

Part of one of the burrows was his—in the miserable slum that he would once have recognised as North Kensington, but which was now little different from anywhere else, save that it was darker.

The taxi stopped. Newman paid, looking up at the distorted face of the immense cliff and trying to remember which entrance at the base he should crawl through to find his burrow.

Habit guided him. He clambered up obsidian slopes to enter the cave-mouth.

It was dark and smelled of damp and old age. A switch clicked beneath his hand but the place remained dark. He headed upwards, climbing slowly, gripping a balustrade he felt rather than saw.

At last he reached his room. Turning on the light, he reeled, for the walls seemed to be at odd angles, and there appeared to be too many surfaces. He made out the gas fire and the ring and the meter, the divan bed, the chest of drawers and the cane-seated chair.

He knew he paid thirty shillings a week for the room and he had lived in it for seven weeks since checking out of a nearby American servicemen's club where he had stayed for a week-end. He had told the club that he was going on to Italy. Per-haps they were looking for him there.

As an astronaut, Newman was a hero and on indefinite leave for having circled the earth umpteen times with his co-pilot, who had died. A steel capsule, cluttered with noisy instru-ments and his space-suited body lying in a semi-horizontal position.

He had had to work hard to get permission to travel around incognito. He had skipped his shadow when he had left the club. He had grown a full beard and let his hair grow longer. He wore dark glasses. His accent was American, but especially unnoticed in the area where he'd chosen to live. Here, nothing about him was particularly peculiar.

Not even his madness, he thought. He was undoubtedly mad, he supposed, though he couldn't believe it absolutely. For some reason he had the feeling that he was somehow seeing things as they actually were. His vision had distorted everything since his return from space, and yet the feeling persisted that, when landing, he had seen everything as it really was for the first time.

Yet the London out there was a madman's London—a dark dream, an ultra-subjective impression and not, as he had sometimes supposed, a super-objective impression.

He staggered towards the bed. Tomorrow he must go out and try to find someone who could help him but wouldn't betray him to the U.S. authorities, who were looking for him. Perhaps others were looking for him, too.

Was all this hallucination? he wondered. Or was it absolute reality—not the apparent reality of conscious life but the reality of the unconscious, the reality which really affected events and controlled society? Was he seeing it as well as sensing it? Or had his senses turned themselves in such a way that images appeared to his conscious mind exactly as they did to his unconscious?

Taking off his overcoat, he lay down on the bed and slept. The London he dreamed of was the London he had passed through in the taxi.

2

IT IS POSSIBLE that Alexander Newman was mad, but when he woke up next morning it was with a feeling of tranquility. Outside, the sun had risen, the pale light reflected on the huge, crooked cliffs that had been the buildings of London. This morning they looked solid and permanent. Newman no longer doubted their reality.

He got off the bed and made his way across the angular room to the gas fire. He lit that and the gas ring and filled a large kettle with water from the tap. When it had boiled he washed himself and felt even more relaxed.

Having breakfasted on milk and cereal, he dressed and went

down the twisted stairs and out into the street, not a gleaming ribbon reminiscent of frozen lava running between the cliffs. A few people passed, their faces quite blank. When he accidentally knocked into one, the man didn't seem to notice. When Newman apologised, the man didn't hear him.

They were like zombies, Newman thought. Like marionettes.

Though the buildings had changed, the general plan of the city had not, and Newman headed towards the Bayswater Road, walking up the narrow, winding gully that had been the Portobello Road. He hardly noticed the girl who walked past him dressed in a farthingale—returning home, possibly, from a late fancy dress party.

Before he reached the end of the street he heard the clang of metal on metal and wondered where the sound came from. Until now he hadn't realised that the silence had been so complete. He turned into a little court, smelling fire and hot steel, and there, in a workshop like a blacksmith's forge, a little man hammered at a beautifully engraved breast-plate from a suit of armour. The man was engrossed in this and Newman watched as he hammered, expertly turning the breast-plate on the anvil with a pair of tongs held in his left hand. The burnished steel shone and glinted in the red light from the fire that burned in the wide grate to the left of the workshop. The armour was covered in small, intricate designs of flowers, crosses and little figures in pastoral settings. It was the design for a lady's sampler rather than for a suit of armour, and the combination of the delicate, embroidery-like design and the martial nature of the thing seemed odd to Newman.

Evidently satisfied at last, the old man straightened up. He was almost as tall as Newman, though his shoulders were stooped and his face had a pink, healthy appearance. He wore glasses and his hair, like his old-fashioned moustache, was thick and white. He gave Newman a genial nod and began to strip off the heavy leather gloves he had worn when working the breast-plate. His apron was also leather, and he now wiped his hands down it to get rid of the sweat.

"Good morning," Newman said. "I don't know anyone like you worked around here."

"You didn't?" The old man smiled. "Good morning. You

aren't a customer, by the look of you."

"How can you tell?"

"I can tell a man who needs armour."

"You're an armourer?"

"That's my trade."

"But surely no one wears armour these days. Only a few ceremonial regiments maybe. Do they employ you?"

The old man shrugged. "Anyone may employ me. Many do. I restore old armour and I make new armour—armour of all kinds, you know. My name is Schweitzer."

"Mine's Newman, Mr. Schweitzer. How do you do?"

"How do you do? Would you like a cup of tea? My wife should have one ready."

"Thanks."

Newman followed the old man through the workshop and entered a dark room behind it—a parlour. It contained a solid table covered with a thick, tasselled tablecloth with a rich, Indian design in purple and gold. An earthenware teapot in a knitted cosy stood on it, steam curling from the spout. There was a small window with dark, velvet curtains and heavy net; a dresser in dark oak held crockery primarily of willow-pattern. Mr. Schweitzer indicated one of two leather armchairs and Newman sat down while Mr. Schweitzer poured the tea into two large mugs.

When they were both sitting, Mr. Schweitzer said: "You seem to have a problem, Mr. Newman. Can I help?"

"I don't think so," Newman said. "I have been confused for some time now, ever since I returned to Earth, but this morning I feel calm. I've a feeling of detachment. You know, of peace—certainty, if you like."

"A very valuable feeling. If all were like you I should be out of work." Mr. Schweitzer smiled and sipped his tea.

"I don't follow you," Newman said.

"I make armour of many sorts, Mr. Newman. Many sorts." Mr. Schweitzer stretched his arm towards the table and put down his cup. "Would you like to see some of the armour I make?"

Newman admitted that he was curious and the old man led him from the parlour, up a narrow staircase and into a store-room, very neatly arranged. Here were shelves and racks bearing a strange assortment of things. There were cards full of pairs of sun-glasses, hats with veils, helmets with visors, a suit of city clothes—black coat, pin-stripe trousers, bowler hat, briefcase and umbrella—on a dummy. There were masks, plain and embroidered and fashioned into grotesque faces; there were Chinese fans, suits of armour from every period of history and every age; there were costumes—crinolines in brown and black, broadcloth suits in black. There were no bright colours among the suits and dresses.

"This is only one section of my stock of armour," Mr. Schweitzer told him. "Call them travelling caves, portable fortresses. But my main stock cannot really be seen."

Puzzled, Newman asked what it was.

"I trade in tangible intangibles, if you like." Schweitzer smiled. "Intangibles that have tangible effects, to be more precise." He went to a bureau and pulled out a drawer full of books. Taking them from the drawer, he spread them before Newman. They were religious books. A Bible, a Koran, the Vestas—all kinds of works by religious thinkers, including modern works.

"I don't understand," said Newman. "This is armour?"

"The most lasting kind, Mr. Newman. It is the armour of *ideas* and of *ritual*. Mental armour to shut out those other ideas..."

"Those are?"

"The ideas we fear, that we refuse to investigate unless swathed in armour. What if there were no purpose to existence, Mr. Newman, other than to exist?"

Newman shrugged. "What of it? That idea does not disturb me."

"I told you I did not think you were a customer of mine. You have the manner of a man who has retreated so far that he has circled right back to the thing he fears—approaching it from the rear, as it were, and finding it not so fearsome as he felt. But that is an unfair judgement. I do not know you."

"You may be right or you may be wrong," Newman answered carelessly. "Even now it occurs to me that I may be totally insane and that you are a figment from my hallucinations."

"What of it? Am I not as real as anything you have known in the past?"

"More so, in many ways."

"Well, then?"

Newman nodded. "I see your point. But could not all this—that transformed city out there, this shop, yourself—could they not be a monstrous suit of armour I have constructed for myself?"

"I am an armourer. I have been in the trade for longer than I would like to say. I know a customer when I see one. You are no customer for me."

"Already you give me reassurance." Newman smiled. "You comfort me with your words—you ease my mind."

"If you say so. There is a difference between self-confidence and self-deception."

"Fair enough." Newman paced around the storeroom, looking at everything. Now that Schweitzer had mentioned it, he could see that it was armour—all of it. It disturbed him that people should go to such lengths to embellish it, to put all their arts and skills into producing it.

There were more books, also—books of attractive, comforting philosophy.

"Antidotes, do you see, Mr. Newman. My job is not to effect cures."

"Just the diving suits," Newman said, picking up a heavy diver's helmet. "So that the depths can be visited but never really explored. And you sell all these?"

"I do not sell them, Mr. Newman. Call me a philanthropist. I give them away." Schweitzer moved towards another door. "This way."

In the next room were large, old-fashioned bottles of the kind once used for keeping sweets. Newman stared at some of the labels. They read: *Cynicism* (J); *Hatred* (M); *Idealism* (R5); *Despair* (12). And so on.

"All armour?" Newman asked.

"Just so. Like the knight who wore that breast-plate you saw me working earlier, people lumber around in their heavy suits and their actions becoming cruder, their movements more sluggish, the longer they wear them. But what can one do? Needs must when the devil drives..."

"And what is the devil, Mr. Schweitzer?"

"Fear. Let us go back to the parlour and see if the tea is still hot enough for a second cup."

While they sat drinking their tea in silence, Newman

thought a little about the things he had seen in Mr. Schweitzer's storerooms. A short time later, the door from the workshop opened and a girl came in. She was very tall and beautiful, wearing no make-up and with long, dark hair framing her face. She wore an ankle-length dress of crimson and both hands held leashes. At the end of one leash was a lyre-bird, very tame and confident, and on the other a peacock with its tail at its peak of splendour, sweeping the ground behind it as it walked beside the girl.

"Good morning, Mr. Schweitzer," she said with a friendly smile. "Is it all right to pop in?"

"Of course, Fanny."

Newman got up.

"This is Miss Fanny Patrick," Schweitzer said. "Mr Newman."

The girl transferred one leash to her left hand and shook hands, giving him the same open smile she had given Schweitzer. "How do you do, Mr. Newman?"

For the first time it struck Newman, not very seriously, that he might have died and entered some previously unimagined heaven or hell—or, more likely, purgatory—since his experiences so far had not affected him particularly strongly in any direction. Fanny Patrick, however, could have come from a dream, for she was, to look at, his ideal woman. What he had seen of her nature seemed to indicate that she was his ideal in this respect as well. He even liked her choice of pets.

"You're not a Londoner, Mr. Newman," she was saying.

"I was born here," he said. "But I went to the States as a kid. I was a space-pilot. I came back to Europe because"—he laughed self-deprecatingly—"because I was looking for some roots, I guess."

"Roots, eh?" She raised an eyebrow. "Geographical?"

"That's what I thought. It all sounds so phoney. Psychological, maybe."

"Have you found them?"

"I'm nor sure. Almost, perhaps."

"That's fine. I'm lunching up the road. Why don't you join me?"

"I'd like to."

"I'd really come to ask Mr. Schweitzer if he felt like an early lunch out," she said, turning to the old man. "What do you say, Mr. Schweitzer?''

''No, thank you.'' Mr. Schweitzer smiled. ''I've some work to get on with. I'm being kept pretty busy at the moment. I'll see you again, Mr. Newman.''

Newman and the girl said goodbye and left through the workshop. The sun was bright and the sky cloudless as they sauntered up the canyon towards a café with a striped awning that jutted out from the cliff-wall on their right. They sat down at one of the tables under the awning and an old, black-clad waiter took their order with a nod of greeting to Fanny Patrick.

''What's your first name?'' she asked as they waited for their food.

''Alexander.''

''Well, there are so few of us here that we tend to get on first-name terms right away. Is that all right by you?''

''Suits me.'' Newman grinned. ''Ah, I feel as though I'm on holiday.''

''You've just got in, have you?''

''I don't quite follow you.''

She smiled. ''I mean, things have changed recently. Your surroundings—that sort of thing.'' She watched as her two birds, which she had freed from their leashes, ran among the tables pecking at scraps of food.

''That's right.''

''It happened to me. I was in a mental hospital for quite a while. Then, one day, everything seemed to sort itself out. The images that I'd kept imagining I saw solidified, if you know what I mean. And here I was. I like it here.''

A thought struck Newman. ''Do you ever get the feeling you should be *doing* something here?''

She shook her head. ''I just take it easy,'' she said. ''There's nothing to do—unless you're someone like Mr. Schweitzer, working for the outside people.''

''Who are they?''

''Almost everybody,'' she said. ''Look, you see that young man walking this way.''

Newman looked and saw him. He was fair-haired, sallow, and his face was somehow tight yet devoid of expression. He walked mechanically, like the people Newman had seen earlier. The other noticeable thing about him was that he was dressed in clothes reminiscent of Edwardian days.

Fanny Patrick got up and walked towards the young man. She shouted "Good morning," but he didn't seem to hear her. She walked alongside him, peering into his face, tapping him gently on the shoulder. A suggestion of vague irritation crossed his face but he walked on without even looking at her. She shrugged, spread her hands and came back to the table.

The young man turned a corner and was out of sight.

"That's the outside people for you, Alexander," she said as she sat down. "Now do you know what I mean?"

"I suppose so. What makes them like that?"

"Oh, too many things."

The lunch came. Newman had ordered schnitzel and noodles; Fanny had a steak diane.

"Those people are still living in the world we knew, is that it?" Newman suggested.

"I suppose it is," she said. "They go in and out of houses, along streets, buy things in shops that are still there as far as they're concerned. Yet we can see that they're not. Two kinds of reality, you see—co-existing. It still comes down to the question, if you care to ask it and worry about it: Is it the minority or the majority who are really insane? Or are all insane?"

3

DRINKING COFFEE after lunch, Fanny Patrick glanced at her watch.

"I'm sailing for Paris this afternoon," she said. "Mustn't miss the ship."

"Paris." Newman was disappointed. "So you're going away."

"Why don't you come, too?" she suggested with a quick smile. "You'd enjoy the voyage. And you've nothing else on, I gather."

"No," he said. "I haven't. But I don't have much money with me and I'd need clothes..." He'd already made up his mind to go if he could.

"Don't worry about either. We don't use money. There's so few of us and we've everything we need. You can get some clothes there."

"All right." He grinned. "I'll come."

"Good. We'll pop back to my place; get my bag, make sure the birds are looked after. That was one reason for calling on Mr. S—his wife usually looks after them for me while I'm away. Then we'll be off."

They left the restaurant and walked round the corner to where a pale section of cliff, like a sandstone butte, stood alone. This was her house. Inside it was spacious, with white walls and red carpets, the furniture of light wood and upholstered in blue. He waited for her in a room which looked out over a landscaped garden with a fountain in the middle. She wasn't long. She came into the room with her bag in her hand, the lyre-bird and the peacock running behind her.

He took the bag.

"I've got a dog-cart ready at the side of the house," she said.

He followed her out to where a scarlet and gold dog-cart, with a palomino pony between its shafts, was waiting for them. She climbed into the seat and lifted the placid birds into the back. Newman got up beside her. She jiggled the reins and the pony moved off.

After they'd left the birds with the pale, pleasant-voiced Mr. Schweitzer, Fanny headed East.

"Where's the boat docked?" he asked.

"Port o'London," she said. "Sailing with the next tide."

London, in spite of its transformation, still seemed brooding and repressive as they made their way through it, but the sun was bright and their mood was good. They passed a few cars, with marionettes at their wheels, and two old people cycling along, the man in plus-fours, the woman in a long, divided skirt. They waved to them cheerfully.

"Not outside people," Newman said, holding on to his seat as the cart gathered speed.

"No, I suppose not. The trouble is, of course, that not so many people of our age seem to get through. They're mostly children or elderly, and the children don't stay long. It's a shame, isn't it?"

"Yes, it is. What about people born here?"

"Children born here are usually taken from their parents after a while. They go outside. Some stay—not many. It's one of the big tragedies—one of the main sacrifices of people who live here."

"It's strange when you think of it," Newman said as they left the canyon that had been Oxford Street and entered another which was High Holborn. "There are traffic jams and jostling crowds here, yet we can't see them and they can't see us. Yet we both exist—we're both solid and real."

"I've often wondered about it," she said. "Are we ghosts? Or do we have an existence in both worlds, just as so many of the outside people do? Perhaps we're corpses lying somewhere in the out-world, eh?"

"I don't like the idea. I can't believe it."

"Neither can I. There's no need to look for explanations, really. Look at that!" She pointed as a man in wig and clothes of the mid-eighteenth century was carried past in a sedan chair by two automata wearing twentieth century clothes. "Have you noticed how time is so mixed up? This is still the twentieth century in most respects, but some people speak and dress like people from as far back as the sixteenth. And here and there you meet people who seem to be from a short way into the future."

"It is surprising," Newman agreed. "It's as if time has sorted itself out into zones where, perhaps, the true mood or event is shown—not in the sequence, or apparent sequence, of the history we knew, but into... well, zones of *influence,* if you like. You know those historians who divide history up into the Age of this and the Age of that. Maybe all the people in this world are from an Age where a particular psychological mood prevailed, dating from around the Renaissance in this case."

"Psychic time zones." She smiled. "Where the nature of the psychic changes very slightly—perhaps even a lot—from zone to zone."

Newman laughed. "Something like that. It all sounds a bit queer." It was odd, he thought, how a conversation like this would not have come at all naturally to him in his other life, yet here it seemed normal.

The pony trotted on through Stepney. The cliffs were blacker and gloomier than ever, with an atmosphere of decay and menace about them. They were like the Mountains of Madness and Newman half-expected ghoulish, flying creatures to come flapping and squawking from their eyries, and to see mis-shapen troglodytes scuttling into cave-mouths, hurling poison-tipped flint spears before disappearing. The sound of the pony's hooves echoed hollowly and Fanny seemed to sense the mood, for she gave the animal its head. It galloped along, and soon the docks were in sight.

The docks were grim and grey, with jagged cliffs stretching along one side and the black river on the other. But the single ship floating at anchor there was in positive contrast to its surroundings. She was a great white clipper ship, her beams bound in bright brass, shining like gold; her sails, as pale as her paint, loose on her four tall masts.

Etched in gold letters on her side was the name, *White Lass*. The dog-cart trundled onto the dockside beside the clipper's main gangplank. An Asiatic sailor, dressed in trim blue jacket and trousers, called to them from the rail.

"Hurry aboard, there—we're sailing within the next five minutes."

They climbed down and walked up the gangplank, Fanny leading the way, Newman behind carrying her bag.

A man in a merchant captain's uniform from around the turn of the century, a clipboard under one arm, came towards them along the deck. He gave them a cheerful salute. He was middle-aged, weather-tanned, and with an imperial beard. His nose was strong and aquiline, his mouth firm and sensitive.

"Good afternoon, captain." Fanny smiled. "Can you take another passenger? This is Mr. Alexander Newman."

"Good afternoon, Miss Patrick—Mr. Newman. Yes, we've plenty of room aboard. You're welcome, sir."

He spoke with a faint foreign accent; a deep voice with a permanent note of warm irony.

"This is Captain Conrad," said Fanny, introducing them. Newman shook hands with him.

"The cabin next to yours is empty," Conrad said. "I think it will suit Mr. Newman, Miss Patrick. You'll excuse me while I get back to work—we're sailing almost at once." He beckoned a white-coated steward who had just emerged from below deck. "Will you put Mr. Newman in the cabin next to Miss Patrick's, please?"

The steward took Fanny's bag from Newman and led them back the way he had come, down a short companionway into a passage which had six doors leading off it, three on each side.

"This is the passenger section," Fanny explained. "The ship is mainly a cargo vessel."

The steward opened one door and took the bag in. Fanny and Newman followed. The cabin was comfortable, with a wide bunk against one bulkhead, a large porthole, washing facilities, a writing desk and a cane chair bolted to the deck under the port-hole and a heavier armchair opposite them.

The steward took Newman out of this cabin and into the one next to it. This was furnished similarly.

"Will that be all, sir?" asked the steward.

"Yes, thanks."

The steward left.

Fanny sauntered into Newman's cabin. "Not bad, eh?" she said. "She's a beautiful ship. You'll realize that most of all when we're on the open sea."

Newman heard shouts above them, felt the ship list very slightly, then right herself.

"They've cast off," Fanny said excitedly. "Come on. Let's go up on deck."

The sails billowed and the ship was soon moving rapidly down river, speeding past the cliffs that were warehouses and rotting buildings, towards open countryside and then the sea.

They joined the captain on the poop deck. He was leaning on a rail and staring down the long river. He looked up with a smile. "Cabins all right?"

"Couldn't be better," said Newman.

"Good."

Newman noticed the silence of the ship as it sailed—just the faint creaking of the rigging. The perpetual noise and smell of even the best steamers was noticeably absent and it seemed a shame to Newman that the clippers, which could match many steamships for speed and capacity, had been abandoned. The slender ship slipped through the water of the river so smoothly that it was almost impossible to tell that they were moving, save for the scenery going past on both sides. Newman saw the helmsman in the wheelhouse behind him, guiding the clipper down the winding strip of water. A bell sounded. Sailors ran about tidying the ship, making lines fast, checking the sails and fastening hatches. The ship was bright, clean and trim, yet with an air of sturdiness about her. She was a fine-looking ship, but it was evident that she could stand hard work, too.

They reached the sea as evening came, the cold, watery flats of the Thames mouth racing by in the waning light; the reeds waving, making the land a parody of the sea.

Now at sea, they left the deck to join the captain in his cabin for supper.

As they ate, Newman said: "This is rather a long way of getting to Paris, isn't it, captain? Normally ships bound for France leave Dover, I thought."

The captain smiled. "Outside, they do, Mr. Newman. But here there are so few ships, and we suit outselves. It is a longer voyage, but we use the rivers as much as we can. On this trip, for instance, we shall be going all the way to Paris, up the Seine. It is longer but simpler, since there are difficulties in getting overland transportation for our cargo and passengers sometimes."

"I can understand now." Newman smiled. "It is a nice way to travel."

"I agree," Fanny said. "We'll cross the sea at night and by morning should have reached the mouth of the Seine. Here, it is possible for ships of this size to sail the big rivers."

In the morning, Newman was awakened by a knock on his door. He called, "Come in," and Fanny entered with some clothes in her arms. There was a pair of jeans and a white shirt, a black, roll-neck jumper and some underwear.

"Captain Conrad managed to sort these out for you," she said. "Will they do? I think they'll fit."

"That's good of him," Newman replied. "They'll be fine."

"I'll see you on deck for breakfast in about half-an-hour," she said as she left.

Newman got up. There was warm water in the taps of the wash-basin and he washed himself all over before drying off and climbing into the clothes Fanny had left. They were a good fit, the waist of the jeans being a little loose, but a broad leather belt answered that problem.

On deck, a small table and two chairs had been set out. Coffee and rolls were on it and Fanny was pouring herself a cup of coffee as he sat down.

The sea was bright blue and the sun exceptionally warm. There was a light wind, sufficient to refresh him and fill the sails of the clipper. Ahead he could see the coast. Captain Conrad called from the poop. "Good morning, you two. Sleep well?"

"Very well," Newman shouted back. "And thanks for the clothes, captain."

"Join me as soon as you've finished breakfast," Conrad invited.

The food was good and the coffee delicious. When they had completed breakfast, they climbed up to the captain's deck. Conrad handed Fanny his field-glasses and she peered through them towards the coast.

"You can just see the mouth of the river," Conrad said, pointing.

Fanny passed the glasses to Newman, who looked through them and saw the river mouth clearly, the tide swirling amongst sandbanks.

"It looks difficult to negotiate," he said, giving the glasses back to Conrad.

"Not when you know it well," the captain replied.

"How long have you been sailing this route, then?" Newman asked.

"A long time, I should think, Mr. Newman. It is difficult to judge the passing of time in this world. The days are of the same duration, but few people bother to count them. The seasons are the same; the tides are the same. Nature does not change, and neither do men and women in this world. They make few attempts to change nature and nature makes few attempts to change them. Time means little here, for that reason as much as anything else."

"You can't remember when you came here?"

"About 1912, I should say."

"And you were the same age then as you are now?"

"I suppose so. I am like a kind of Flying Dutchman, eh?" Conrad laughed. "Except I am very happy with my situation."

"You feel no regret—no boredom?"

"I don't think so. I was once a man of action. I played my part in the world, as you once did. But not any more. Perhaps I should feel uncomfortable about the kind of life I lead now, but I don't."

"But you play a part in this world. What is this world?"

"It is the real world as seen by the inner mind, Mr. Newman. The real world as seen by the outer mind is the one you left. The inner mind is the true mirror of human history, in my opinion. It is the inner mind that creates the ideas that produce the great events, the outer mind translates them into action—deals with the details, you might say. Yet when the outer mind tries to interpret these events that it has helped produce, it always fails. It always finds anomalies, puzzles—while to the inner mind everything is clear. That is the irony of it."

"The outer mind needs the inner mind, then?"

"They are complementary. We know which controls what, but the important thing is which controls the individual. The majority of people pay too little attention to the inner mind, allowing their judgements to be swayed by the apparent logic of the outer mind. That is where they go wrong."

"But aren't we just as guilty, obeying the inner mind too completely?"

"Perhaps. I only know what I prefer to do."

Newman was in a quandary for the first time since he had come here.

"Has this world no future, then?" he asked. "No future of its own?"

"Apparently not. A few things change from time to time, depending on where you are, but there is no progress in the terms of the outer mind. It's strange, really, for only the inner mind is unaffected by the passing of time—or affected very little, at least. Yet only the inner mind can predict, in general ways, the future as it is likely to be. It can plot a rough course; it can even judge which winds are likely to change, and when. But it does not care. That is left to the outer mind, for the outer mind produces the actions after the inner mind has supplied the original impulse."

"Then should there not be a balance?" said Newman.

"Ideally, Mr. Newman. But this is not an ideal world. We are lucky, the few of us here, to have the choice."

The Seine flowed through rich countryside which was picturesque even for the season. It was entirely rural, with no towns sighted until Paris came in view.

Newman had expected something similar to London, but he

had been wrong.

Paris was a city of coloured crystal, a dazzling piece of gigantic yet delicate jewellery from which light blazed. Newman was delighted. "Magnificent!" he said to Fanny, who stood beside him by the rail of the main deck. "I never imagined anything so beautiful. It's like a heavenly city." He laughed. "Will Saint Peter let us in, do you think?"

She smiled back, tucking her arm in his. "I don't think there'll be much difficulty, Alexander."

The *White Lass* sailed into Paris a short while later, her whole deck alive with the light from the city, the water sparkling with a thousand rejected colours. Tall poplars grew along the banks of the river and the buildings were not the bleak cliffs of London but great structures of multi-coloured crystal, with tall spires and turrets and domes.

They docked. Fanny and Newman thanked Captain Conrad and disembarked.

"They love glory, the French." Fanny grinned as they walked through the avenues while the city seemed almost to sing with colour and light. "This city is like their music— delightful yet, you suspect, insubstantial. Romantic, rather grandiose, beautiful but artificial—like their philosophy and their art. And like all those things," she smiled, pretending to shied her eyes, "it is dazzling."

"You seem to have a great affection for the French."

"So I have. They treat serious things lightly and light things seriously. This makes them amusing and, to the Anglo-Saxon, refreshing. What other race could make a profound philosophy of the obvious?"

4

THE CRYSTAL CITY was entrancing. They wandered through it hand in hand as Fanny showed Newman the sights.

Although the faceted structures were not recognizable as any buildings Newman had ever known, they had the grace and inspiration of great architecture. Yet, like London's black stone cliffs, they seemed natural phenomena rather than man-made. They were, at least in one sense, man-made, for, like London, they represented an ideal of a city. Newman reflected on the nature of the average Londoner that he should desire the cave dwellings and gloomy abysses rather than a city like Paris, alive with colour and light. The broad avenues were tree-lined and there were a few more people about than there had been in London, though the marionette population from the 'outside' were still primarily in evidence.

Having lunched inside one of the crystal buildings—all gilt, plush and big mirrors, with waiters in white aprons and black suits reminiscent of the '90s—Newman and Fanny wandered out until they came to a wide square full of topiary animals and birds, cathedrals and famous figures from French history, all exquisitely cut from the shrubs. In miniature lakes, fountains of ormolu and precious metals, marble and delicately painted enamel, played the water coloured like rainbows. And from a small pavilion some distance away, its little roof of red, white and blue stripes, its supports of gilded iron, twisted like barley sugar sticks, bunting looped between them, came music. There sat a string quartet with a French horn player, their music on stands in front of them. As Newman and Fanny drew nearer, Newman recognized Mozart's E flat Quintet for French horn and strings, its wit and humanity at once blending and contrasting with the surroundings in which it was being played.

The performers were dressed in clothes contemporary with Mozart—fine silk coats, embroidered waistcoats, lacy shirts and elaborate wigs. They might have been performing for the last of the Bourbons at Versailles.

A few people, one or two dressed like the performers but most of them in different styles of the twentieth century, stood around the pavilion listening to the music. Newman and Fanny joined them.

When the piece was finished the performers stood up and bowed as the listeners applauded. They had played magnificently. They stepped down from the pavilion and began to chat with the others. Newman had expected to hear them talking in the flowery speech of eighteenth century France. Instead, he was astonished at their accents, which were evidently American.

Newman approached the horn player. "Are you from the States?" he asked in English.

"Sure, man." The horn player nodded. "But we'd better

Michael Moorcock

talk French here, if it's okay with you. These guys don't like anything else."

"You played very well," Newman said in French. "That was the best playing of Mozart chamber music I ever heard."

"Good of you to say so. They seem to like our way of playing too. Excuse me." The horn player pointed across the park to where a Renault had drawn up. The driver was waving to them. "We've got another engagement. Hope to see you again."

The musicians, their instruments and music under their arms, walked through the park to the car, climbed in and the car drove away.

At length, almost everyone else had gone, apart from three men, who stopped to chat with Fanny. One of them was dressed in the elaborate clothes of the eighteenth century; another wore the heavy, respectable high-crowned hat, frock-coat and dark trousers of the Second Empire, while the third had on black, tight-fitting trousers, a black pullover and had a black beret on his thick hair. A thin cigarette was between his lips. He looked something like an *apache,* or a caricature of one.

"I think I prefer Debussy," the man in the bright silk coat was saying. "There is something just a trifle *heavy,* even in Mozart."

"I can't say I agree," Fanny replied with a smile. "This is my friend, Alexander Newman. He's an American, too."

"Delighted," said the three men as they shook hands with Newman.

"What did you think of your cousins' performance?" asked the man in the top hat.

"Brilliant," said Newman. "No doubt about it."

"Mmm, perhaps. Myself, I felt it was rather insufficiently restrained."

"You would think that, Berger," said the man in the beret, slapping him on the back. "Restraint in all things for you, eh?"

"Just so, M. Alfred."

"I wonder if M. Sol agrees," Berger said, turning to the man in the eighteenth century finery. "What do you think, Sol? Not restrained enough for you—the performance?"

"It was too restrained. A little more flair was called for, I felt," Sol replied with a faint smile.

They could have been brothers. Their complexions were dark, their lower lips protuberant, their noses large, their eyelids heavy and expression deliberately controlled. With an exchange of clothes they might have been the same man.

"Ah, well." Alfred smiled. "Enough of this. Let's have some wine at my place. Will you join us, ma'amoiselle—M'sieu?"

"Certainly," said Fanny, "if you'll have us."

"Come, then."

They all followed Alfred from the park and up an avenue, in through a door of rose-coloured glass into a passageway lined with gilt-framed mirrors that were a little fly-specked and their gilt rather faded.

A quaint lift-cage of rococo ironwork took them up several stories and then they were in Alfred's room. It was lit by a large skylight that almost covered one wall and the roof. A mattress lay against the far wall, its blankets untidy. On it lay a girl staring blankly upwards. A table was covered with pages of manuscript and books. Several bottles of rosé stood on it.

"Oh, Alfred!" Berger said, pointing at the girl. "How could you do that?"

Newman thought Berger was shocked at finding a woman in Alfred's room, but then he noticed that the girl had the dazed, set expression of an 'outsider'.

"Why not?" Alfred said lightly. "After all, we can manipulate them sometimes if we wish to. Yesterday I wished to. And what will she know about it?"

"It is not done to disturb these people," Mr. Sol said. "You know that, Alfred. Who do you think you are to justify this? How would you justify it? With the logic of a de Sade?"

Alfred shrugged. "I'll get rid of her, then. Take care of the wine, will you, Sol?" He stooped, lifted the girl in his arms and carried her out.

Sol gave them all wine and, when Alfred returned, handed him a glass.

The atmosphere was strained for a while, but the wine helped to restore everyone to better spirits.

"Is this you first visit to Paris, M. Newman?" Berger asked. He had taken off his top hat and placed it on a chair beside him.

"The first under these conditions," Newman replied. "I'm impressed. In London I was convinced that the images that reached the... the 'inner mind', were wholly depressing. I was wrong. Paris is a miracle."

"And what do you think of France in general?"

"I have only been here a few hours."

"But the French," M. Sol said, waving a hand at the window as if the French were waiting outside to hear Newman's judgement. "The French. You must have an opinion of us. Everyone has."

"Just as we have an opinion of everyone," said Alfred with a smile.

Rising to the occasion, Newman said: "I find the French charming, the architecture breathtaking and the public transport bewildering. The museums are magnificent, the exhibits, on the whole, mediocre. The French are the gentlest and the roughest people in the Western world. They are absolutely courteous—and absolutely ill-mannered."

"Never 'absolute'!" whispered M. Sol in mock horror. "Never that, m'sieu!"

"What do you mean?"

Fanny laughed. "Yes, what do you mean, M. Sol?"

"The Frenchman knows of the absolute, ma'amoiselle, but he despises it," Alfred interjected.

"Exactly," said Sol. "It is the curse of the French that they will go to extremes. We form a republic and then worship an emperor. We have been doing it for nearly two hundred years. Republic, emperor—republic, emperor. Sometimes we call them by different names. Yet the Frenchman claims to avoid extremes and never to approach the absolute. But we are a nation of enthusiasts. When an idea fires us we put all we have into it. When it bores us we abandon it. But we are not sufficiently obsessive to stick at one thing for long. Our ambitions are short-lived. That is why we lose wars and art never reaches the great, grim heights you Anglo-Saxons demand. We have become afraid of excess, m'sieu. M. Berger, as you noticed this afternoon, distrusts any hint of it. Yet give him a mission for a day or so and he would show you what excess really meant!" Sol laughed.

"Nonsense," said Berger, looking embarrassed.

Alfred laughed, too. Drunkenly. He swayed around the

room, refilling everyone's glass. He kept blinking.

"Do not drink so much," Berger said to him. "You will go back."

"My will is too strong." Alfred bellowed as he fell on to his mattress.

"We shall see," Berger murmured.

Newman began to feel uncomfortable. He looked at Fanny, trying to see if she were ready to leave, but she made no sign. She seemed to be enjoying herself.

Alfred shook his head dazedly. "I am an intellectual," he said. "I am the life-blood of France."

"Nonsense," Berger said. "It is the intellectuals who have ruined France. It is the bourgeoisie who have tried to sustain her."

"It is the aristocrats who have managed to," Sol put in. "Every time France flounders she finds a new élite. The Bourbons, Napoleon, de Gaulle and so on... What else do you expect of a paternalistic nation? It must be so."

Alfred rose, staggered to his desk, opened a drawer and took out a revolver. "And so must this be so!" he shouted waving it.

"Not these days, surely," Sol murmured sardonically.

Fanny got up. "M. Alfred, is the gun loaded?"

"It is, ma'amoiselle," he said with a drunken bow. He pointed it at his head. She reached out hastily to take it, but he staggered back, his arm falling. Again he began to blink rapidly. His other hand went to his temple and squeezed it. "Ah! You are right, Berger. I must stop drinking."

"Why do you do it—this drinking to excess?" Berger seemed perturbed and worried for his friend. "And the girl? Why are you so irresponsible towards your own fate and everyone else's?"

"Curiosity," Sol remarked. "Isn't that so, Alfred? Curiosity?"

"Yes, yes." Alfred wandered back to the mattress.

"He is not merely content to be in this ideal world," Sol said, turning to Newman and Fanny. "He must investigate it always—test it. He ruins what could be a perfectly good and long life. Can you believe it?"

Newman felt some sympathy with Alfred. He was the first man he had met here who seemed to be dissatisfied with the 'inner world'.

"There could be something in what he is trying to do," Newman suggested. "Living here is like a perpetual holiday. There's nothing to do when you get here. It's nice for a while, but..."

"But then you want to start spoiling it," Berger said heatedly. "Others have tried without success. Most of them have died or gone back. Think of that! Dying and leaving heaven!"

"Be content," Sol said. "Relax and be content. It is this contentedness which should mark us from the others 'outside'."

"It makes us superior?" Newman asked.

"Of course it does. Have you something against superiority?"

"I don't believe it."

"Do not try to pursue your American ideal of equality here, my friend," Sol mocked. "Look where it has led your nation—to a greater degree of inequality than exists anywhere else in the Western world."

"At present," Newman agreed. "Besides, the American ideal of equality is that every man should be a king. A king must have subjects so, unfortunately, it means that every king must try to become an emperor. But that will change, I think."

"Let it. It will not affect us here very much."

"Don't be too sure," Newman said. "The only difference between us and them is that we recognize and control the inner mind. But those out there still possess those inner minds —and they still represent a force to be reckoned with, for they can take action. What sort of action can be taken here that will affect the destiny of mankind?"

"Mankind has no destiny but to exist." Alfred had risen from the mattress again, the revolver still in his hand. "All that the inner mind is, is a survival mechanism that controls his actions, makes them fit the pattern of the universe, though this is not always observable in the outer world. The inner mind makes him behave in accordance with the laws of nature, though his outer mind would attempt to thwart those laws and thus destroy him. The inner mind is in tune with the rhythm of the spheres, gentlemen. As individuals we are nothing and as a race we simply exist. That is our only purpose. Why should we seek another? The inner mind does not seek another. We do not seek another here.''

''And if one cannot believe it?'' Newman enquired.

''Then you have no business being here!'' Sol stood up. ''He is right. You know he is right.''

''He *is* right, Alexander,'' said Fanny. ''I'm sure of it.''

''So am I,'' Newman said. ''And I suspect anything I'm so sure of. I think of Mr. Schweitzer's armour.''

''You are in a worse position than Alfred,'' Berger said with a sidelong glance at Sol. He winked.

There was a shot. Alfred was falling, the gun clattering to the floor, his eyes staring as he pitched forward.

''The fool,'' Sol said casually. ''He has denied his purpose. He has thwarted his destiny. He has ceased to exist!''

Fanny began to sob and Newman tried to comfort her.

M. Sol sighed. ''What do we do now, Berger? This is upsetting. I feel a trifle uncomfortable. What does one do in such a time of crisis?''

Berger began to take off his jacket. ''Change clothes, M. Sol. It is all there is to do.''

Beside the corpse of Alfred, the two men began to strip off their clothes and trade them. Soon Sol was dressed in Berger's frock-coat, trousers and top hat, and Berger wore Sol's silks and lace. Newman was horrified by the charade and watched speechlessly as Fanny sobbed on and the pair left the room.

''Let's get away from here, Alexander,'' Fanny said a little later. ''Poor M. Alfred. It was so unexpected.''

Newman helped her out to the lift. As they descended, he said. ''Do you want to leave Paris altogether, then?''

''Don't you?''

''I wouldn't mind.''

''I have a car near here. We can leave right away.''

''Where shall we go?''

''I don't care. Just drive.''

The car was a big, old Citroen limousine. Newman found it easy to handle. He drove through the streets of the crystal city. Fanny staring blankly ahead.

Soon they were in the countryside, heading north.

5

NEWMAN DROVE for more than a day along a wide, straight road that went on and on between flat fields. He didn't know where it led, and he didn't care. He was trying to think and finding thinking difficult.

It was on the second day of living off raw vegetables found in the fields and sleeping in the car that they saw a van ahead of them, driving in the same direction.

By this time Fanny had cheered up a little. When she saw the van she brightened even more.

"Alexander! It's Mr. Schweitzer's van. I wonder where he's going."

Relieved at the prospect of seeing a familiar face, Newman accelerated, passing the van with a wave as he saw Mr. Schweitzer in the cabin.

Schweitzer smiled, looking a trifle puzzled, and pulled into the side of the road.

Newman backed the Citroen up to the van and helped Fanny out. They reached the van as Mr. Schweitzer climbed down.

"What are you two doing here?" he asked. "I thought you'd gone to Paris."

"We decided to leave," Newman told him. He described what had happened.

Schweitzer shook his head and pursed his lips, sighing.

"Yes, yes. That sometimes does happen. In France especially. They shun my wares there, you know, but they need them, really..."

"They need something," said Fanny earnestly.

"Where does this road lead?" Newman asked. "We've no idea."

"It leads to Berlin, Mr. Newman. I don't think you want to go there."

"Why not?"

"It's an unpleasant place at the best of times. A strange place. My biggest single customer, you know. Why don't you turn round—go back to Paris or take a side road to Amsterdam or Hamburg and see if you can find a ship to get you to London?"

"I'm curious now," Newman smiled. "I think I'd like the experience of Berlin, Mr. Schweitzer."

"I suppose it can do you little harm, Mr. Newman. Very well. If you'd like to keep pace with my old van, we'll travel together."

They followed the road for the rest of the day and at night camped beside it. Mr. Schweitzer was well equipped with a primus stove and provisions. They ate well for the first time since they had left Paris.

They slept in the tent Mr. Schweitzer lent them and at dawn were on the road again.

A few hours later they sighted Berlin.

There was a vast wall surrounding the city and it was really this they sighted rather than Berlin itself, which was completely hidden by the wall.

Its black, basalt sides were high and smooth and small gateways led through from the roads.

As they neared it, Newman could make out figures high above on the top of the wall. The figures were encased in full medieval armour; from head to foot they were dressed in metal, holding sub-machine guns cradled in their arms.

"Here the whole city is populated by those who see with the inner eye," Schweitzer explained. "But what their inner eye see—its ideal... Oh dear! This Berlin—it is the City of Fear. Such a strange people—so perceptive yet so terrified. They warp their perceptions even as they find them. A dreadful mix-up, I'm afraid."

The guards seemed to recognize Schweitzer's van, for the doors of the gateway were swung open and they passed through into the city.

Berlin was smaller than London in every respect, but what Newman hadn't noticed was that the whole city had a roof, stretching from wall to wall. The roof was of heavy, smoked glass, or something similar, and it let in too little light.

Many of the buildings looked like huge, round boulders with tiny entrances, just about big enough for a man to crawl through.

Michael Moorcock

The streets, like the tunnels of some stone maze, were full. Lumbering horses bore the great, clumsy weight of armoured men, while others, on the pavements, wore masks or heavy hoods to hide their faces.

The van was forced to stop in a small square, for it could not negotiate the narrow streets.

They got out. A man in a 1914-18 flying suit, with fur jacket, boots and gauntlets, but wearing a Gothic helmet on his head, the visor covering his face, walked towards Schweitzer, hand held out.

His voice was an echo in the helmet when he spoke in German, a language which Newman understood only imperfectly. After shaking hands with the man, Schweitzer introduced Newman and Fanny as English.

"Herr von Richthofen, eh?" Newman said. "Any relation to the Baron?"

Von Richthofen shrugged. "We don't use those titles in our Germany, Herr Newman. Would you like to come back to my house for some refreshment?"

The house was one of a number of boulders on the far side of the square. They entered it, having to stoop through the small doorway. Inside it was, if anything, gloomier than outside. A few torches illuminated a fairly large hall and a fire glimmered in a grate. A stone-staircase led upwards and von Richthofen climbed it until they entered a smaller, slightly more hospitable room, heated, it appeared, by some sort of steam apparatus. Newman sat down on a wet chair, coughing as the hot, damp air entered his lungs. The place was like a Turkish bath and there was a faint smell of salt around.

"Some food will be brought to us," von Richthofen said. "Well, Herr Schweitzer, what have you got this time? Heavier stuff than last, I hope. The fashions change so rapidly and now one must wear an even thicker plate than ever if one is to fit in." He reached up and lifted off his ornate steel helmet. The face revealed was of a man of about thirty-five—handsome, self-indulgent, faintly cynical.

"That's better," he said. "I only feel comfortable with it off in here."

Newman looked around. There were no windows in the room. It seemed very strange to him and he could not imagine why people should choose to live in such places.

The food arrived. Dull, German food—sausages, saurkraut, bread, but good coffee.

When they had eaten, von Richthofen leant back in his wooden armchair.

"Have you just come from England, Herr Newman?"

"No. I was in Paris first."

"Paris! A wonderful city. Very romantic. You liked it?"

"In general. It seems strange that you should like it, Herr von Richthofen, when your own taste in architecture is so different."

"Aha! So very different, eh? But *secure*, do you see, Herr Newman? Strong, invincible, able to withstand anything."

Newman was puzzled. "But why should it be? Are you expecting trouble? Who'd attack you?"

"We do not know. But better safe than sorry, eh?"

Newman, the damp having penetrated his clothing, shifted uncomfortably on his chair. "I suppose so."

Von Richthofen seemed to notice his discomfort. He laughed. "You get used to that. Oh, we know all about freedom and beautiful surroundings making beautiful minds. All that sort of thing. But we have made a conscious sacrifice. A study of history will show you that a race of a group which holds firmly together, building heavy walls, survives longer than one which lives in idyllic surroundings. Look at Greece. Compare it with Rome. You see what I mean?"

Newman didn't. He thought von Richthofen was misguided. He could see no logic in what the man was saying.

"I should have thought that here, in the inner world, you would not need such walls or such ideas. Your walls are built because you fear something—something which you do not know exists. Living in this world, you surely realize this?"

"We realize that you are probably right. But there is a possibility that you are wrong. It is that possibility we prepare for, Herr Newman. The German is capable of mental detachment more than anyone. That is why you find so many of us here in Berlin—a whole city of us."

"But you use this detachment to escape, it seems to me," Newman said. "Some people read adventure stories. Not you —you invent complicated systems of metaphysics. And you achieve the same end. You leave reality."

"Is not our reality the same as yours—on the inner or the

outer plane?''

"It borders on it. But is your fortified city 'realistic' in this world? Is your fashion for wearing heavier armour 'realistic'? Surely these are totally subjective things. I find it very difficult to understand how these things, so typical of the outer world, can exist in the inner world. I remember reading of some Crusaders once who went across the desert to fight a battle. They refused to dispense with their armour, in spite of crippling heat and utter weariness. They rode for days, until all sense of reality was driven from them. Finally, harried all the way by Saracens, they reached their battle-ground and were trapped and massacred. If only they had taken their armour off to cross the desert they would have done so at greater speed and arrived fresh. Because of their *need* for their armour— which *reason* told them they did not need—they perished. Their armour killed them, in fact.''

Von Richthofen pursed his lips ironically. "A nice little moral tale, Herr Newman. But we Germans are different. We see things in a far bigger way. We do not just take the world view—we take the universal view.''

"How does that bear on what we're discussing?''

"It has every bearing. Every bearing.''

Von Richthofen got up. "I would like some time to show you what Athens has become.''

"I've never been to Athens,'' Fanny put in. "What has it become?''

Von Richthofen put his hand to his chin. "You want to know? Very well, I will fly you there myself—tomorrow. When we have seen what Mr. Schweitzer has to offer us. How would you like that?''

Newman was willing to take any opportunity to leave Berlin as speedily as possible. "Suits me,'' he said. "I'd like to go to Greece. It's one of my favourite countries.''

"Is it, Herr Newman? Is it? Good.''

6

VON RICHTHOFEN'S PLANE was very modern. It lay on an airfield outside the walls of Berlin. It resembled an American Phantom fighter-bomber in almost every detail. On its wings and fuselage, however, were painted large swastikas.

"They are just for old times' sake," von Richthofen said with a laugh as he led them up to the plane. They were all dressed in pressure suits. They had just said goodbye to Mr. Schweitzer. "A joke, you know," Richthofen added. "I feel no embarrassment these days. Do you?"

Newman said nothing. He helped Fanny into the big cockpit, wider than a Phantom's. It could take three—two in the front and one just behind. Expertly, he settled himself into his own seat. He had flown similar aircraft before he began training for space.

Von Richthofen started the engine and at length the plane began to move off down the long runway. They were quickly airborne and von Richthofen, for Fanny's sake, kept the speed down to just over the speed of sound.

They flashed through the peaceful sky at four thousand feet, heading south-east for Greece.

They landed on a long airstrip just outside Athens. There were none of the usual airport buildings, just the tarmac with grassy slopes on either side.

Newman was surprised to see that Athens was not the modern city but the ancient one transformed. Graceful villas, widely spaced, surrounded tree-lined squares. Here and there were larger buildings, like the Parthenon and the Acropolis. Most of the people wore togas or linen jerkins tied loosely at the waist. The women wore the flowing robes that Newman had previously only seen represented on statues, paintings or bas reliefs. But there were several who wore the clothes of other periods, including Newman's own.

The sun was warm and the mood of the city leisurely. A few people waved cheerfully to them, but most were gathered in little groups, lazing in the sun, drinking wine and eating fruit and talking all the time. The hum of conversation filled the city.

"It hasn't been changed," Newman said to von Richthofen. "Why is that?"

"There has been no need, my friend. This Athens is the Athens of the Golden Age, altered in only minor details. Here the idea and the actuality are one. Here, the inner mind and the outer mind merged to produce an idea. It happens rarely. The cities you have seen so far—London, Paris, Berlin—are transformed because the idea the builders had of them was never fulfilled in actuality. Only an approximation was produced. Not so with the Athenians. It took later ages to spoil the ideal city—later events. But events have not altogether changed the Greeks as they changed us Northerners. Time has not 'moved on' so much." Von Richthofen laughed unpleasantly. "But they are not strong, Herr Newman—Fraulein Patrick."

"They don't need to be *strong*," Fanny said in bewilderment, putting her arm through Newman's. "What have they to fear here?"

"Only the inconsistent—only some arbitary action disobeying the fundamental laws of existence. We of the inner world all recognise these laws, I believe."

"And they are?" Fanny said.

"Simple. That nature follows a pattern—a simple cycle of birth, death and rebirth. Everything obeys this law, from the tiniest particles to the suns and galaxies of the infinite universe. But, basically, everything remains the same—everything is consistent, fixed forever according to the pattern."

"It simply exists, is that it?" Newman said, remembering the words of the late M. Alfred. "It had no purpose but to exist."

"Exactly. So your Parisians exist in their crystal city, in their still somewhat artificial way. Here, in Athens people exist in a simpler, more natural way. This is right, you say; this is proper. This obeys the law of the universe."

"Fair enough," said Fanny. "But what are you driving at?"

"I am trying to tell you what we Berliners protect ourselves against in this perfect inner world, Fraulein Patrick. All you have seen here so far—apart from our Berlin—have accepted that to live without fear, without protection and suspicion, is *moral*—that is, it accords with the true pattern of existence."

"Okay," said Newman. "What about it?"

"Have you never considered that detachment of the kind we have might recognise that law, might understand the essential morality of our Greek friends here—but decide coolly, out of pure whim, *to disobey the law and live immorally?* A man or a group of men might decide to 'throw a spanner in the works', *ja*! Out of boredom, perhaps—out of despair or out of curiosity? We are ultimately bound by the law, Herr Newman, but that does not stop us from *consciously* disobeying it. To recognise the invulnerable and eternal law is not automatically to obey it. Do you see? We are conscious, reasoning beings—we can *decide* to disobey."

"But what point would there be in doing that?" Fanny asked, bemused. "In the outer world the law is broken all the time—insensately, out of fear and greed and bewilderment. That's understandable. But here, who would break the law?"

"You ask what point is there in doing such a thing." Von Richthofen smiled. "But there again what point is there in existence? None. To make one's mark, however small, one can only behave illogically in an ultimately logical universe. Who are the great myth figures of our history? Disrupters all! Even where they preached the law they succeeded in producing more chaos than had existed before they came. Here, in this inner world, we are all equal. Supposing a man achieved this plan and refused to accept what he found. Suppose he deliberately offended against the law of the universe. What then?"

"This is the possibility you fear in Berlin?" Newman said quietly. "This?"

"Why should we not fear it in Berlin? Haven't we sufficient cause to do so? Is not our history full of the servants of chaos?"

"And of order, too. Your composers—Bach, in particular—a rarity—a totally sane genius. Your poets, your novelists—Thomas Mann, for one. Goethe, Brecht."

"Just so. We have the ability, as I told you, to *see*—but there are those amongst us who are not content with seeing—they wish to take action in a world that denies action, other than those necessary for existence alone, and demands the *status quo*."

"You sound like one yourself." Newman smiled half-heartedly.

Von Richthofen shrugged. "I am not the stuff of the anti-Christ," he said. "I only try to illustrate what Berlin still fears; detachment, vision, knowledge do not bring an automatic absence of danger."

"You mean that what people say in the outer world—about if everyone could achieve detachment, rise above themselves, everything would be better? You mean that's not necessarily true?" said Fanny.

"Why should it be?"

"Why, indeed..." Newman agreed. "But you serve no good to yourselves or others by wrapping yourselves in stone and metal, and hiding."

Richthofen smiled. "It is our duty. We obey the universal, fundamental law."

"How?" Newman asked.

"We exist—and we see to it that we continue to exist. But enough of this. I came here not only to tell you what I meant, but to illustrate my point." He took something from the pocket of his flying suit. Then he threw back his arm and flung the object towards the Parthenon. "Witness," he said. "The arbitary action."

He must have thrown a grenade.

The Parthenon blew up, bodies were scattered, many torn to pieces. Greeks came hurrying on to the scene, absolutely shocked, almost incapable of action. Slowly, a few began to go to the aid of the wounded.

Newman and Fanny were horrified. "Murder..." whispered Newman.

"Murder, yes. Call it what you will. Suppose such a man as myself came to Berlin. He would do little harm."

Von Richthofen turned around with a crooked smile on his face and began to walk casually away from the destruction. Nobody tried to stop him.

"I'm returning to Berlin now," he said. "Do you want to come? You'll be welcome."

"I'll take my chances," Newman said grimly, his mind reeling. "What about you, Fanny?"

"Me, too," she said.

Around them, Athens was fading and soon all they could see

was the ruin of the Parthenon. The airfield had gone; so had von Richthofen and his jet.

"We're back," Fanny said faintly. "Aren't we, Alexander?"

"I think so."

"What do we do now?"

"We've got to do something," he said. "I suppose." They walked away from the ruin of the Parthenon towards the other Athens.

(Colville Terrace, W.11, 1965.)

SavoyBooks

in association with New English Library Ltd

Cover photo by Ron Sumner

● COMPLETE BOOK LIST ● NEW RELEASES

SAVOY·SAVOY·SAVOY·SAVOY· 1980

Michael Moorcock

THE RUSSIAN INTELLIGENCE
(193mm x 125mm)

Jerry Cornell is the exact opposite of a super sleuth.
Always careful to choose a case that will solve itself
so he can spend most of his agency's time in bed with
his bird. But his luck runs out when he accidentally
takes on the assignment codenamed DEVIL RIDER.
The hilarious, detective thriller sequel to *The Chinese
Agent*. Illustrated by Harry Douthwaite.

160pp £1.25 Paperback ISBN 0 86130 027 0

SOJAN
(193mm x 125mm)

Moorcock's first Sword & Sorcery hero now in print
for the first time in 20 years. The Warrior Lord Sojan
battles on a strange and remote planet, his heroic
adventures setting the stage for all Moorcock's later
champions. The book contains definitive articles by
the author on Jerry Cornelius and the secret life of
Elric of Melniboné. Illustrated by James Cawthorn.

160pp £0.80 Paperback ISBN 0 86130 000 9

MY EXPERIENCES IN
THE THIRD WORLD WAR . . .
(193mm x 125mm)

The new Savoy Michael Moorcock release for
1980. This original collection of fictional
reminiscences, each segment revolving around
the interlinking theme of the Third World
War, is a powerful emotive work.

176pp £1.50 Paperback ISBN 0 86130 037 8

THE GOLDEN BARGE
(210mm x 148mm)

Pursuing an impossible goal and hounded by dark
dreams which drive him to cold-hearted murder,
Jephraim Tallow seeks the meaning of life in a wild
and intense world. Moorcock's first anti-hero predates
the creation of Elric of Melniboné by 12 months in a
classic novel that combines the elements of
symbolism and fantasy as masterfully as Peake or
T. H. White. The high quality, 3-D "Videoback"
packaging of this very first Michael Moorcock novel
follows Savoy's trendsetting design for *Phoenix
Without Ashes* by Harlan Ellison. Illustrated by James
Cawthorn.

224pp £1.25 Videoback ISBN 0 86130 002 5

Michael Moorcock

Samuel Delany

Harlan Ellison

Henry Treece

James Cawthorn

Jack Trevor Story

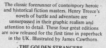

Henry Treece

The classic forerunner of contemporary heroic and historical fiction masters. Henry Treece's novels of battle and adventure are unsurpassed in their graphic realism and attention to detail. These four great editions are now released for the first time in paperback in the UK. Illustrated by James Cawthorn.

THE GOLDEN STRANGERS
(Introduced by Michael Moorcock)
(193mm x 125mm)

Set at a vital cross-roads in history, this is the story of a young prince of the dawn world – Garroch – who tries to repel the invasion of Britain by the Golden Strangers.

224pp £1.25 Paperback ISBN 0 86130 018 1

THE DARK ISLAND
(Introduced by Michael Moorcock)
(193mm x 125mm)

A further novel of Britain, set during the Roman invasion before Christianity has asserted itself, and when the island is torn and divided by successive raiders from abroad.

240pp £1.25 Paperback ISBN 0 86130 021 1

RED QUEEN, WHITE QUEEN
(Introduced by Michael Moorcock)
(193mm x 125mm)

Red Queen, White Queen takes place before the collapse of Rome, when Queen Boadicea rises against the might of the Imperial Legions to become the true, if brief Queen of the British people.

240pp £1.25 Paperback ISBN 0 86130 020 3

THE GREAT CAPTAINS
(Introduced by Michael Moorcock)
(193mm x 125mm)

This is the story of King Arthur as it may really have happened. A superb novel of the wild, forbidding world of ancient Britain.

240pp £1.25 Paperback ISBN 0 86130 019 X

Illustrations by James Cawthorn.

Available for the first time in paperback . . .
A FIGHTING MAN
(193mm x 125mm)

A Fighting Man depicts the Regency England of the West Midlands with startling force. The action centres on one Ned Ashton and his adventures as a prize-fighting man, and portrays all too vividly the brutality of prize-fighting which itself reflected a viscious age. Illustrated by James Cawthorn.

240pp £1.50 Paperback ISBN 0 86130 050 5

THE REBELS
(193mm x 125mm)

Set in the Black Country during the late 19th Century, Henry Treece brings this novel of the fortunes of a middle class family in Victorian Staffordshire as vividly alive as Celtic Britain in his previous books. Ambitiously constructed, *The Rebels* is one of the most unusual and individual works of Henry Treece's career. Illustrated by James Cawthorn

240pp £1.50 Paperback ISBN 0 86130 049 1

The Tides of Lust
(193mm x 125mm)

In this salacious but profoundly penned erotic odyssey, million selling author, Samuel Delany charts the search for erogenous gratification of a diverse collection of people. Fantastic erotics and unheard-of-evil are beautifully orchestrated by Delany, who tells of an astonishing range of permutations in language that is at once photographic, poetic and unexpected – in the classic erotic tradition of *Story of O, The Pearl* and Philip José Farmer's *Image of the Beast*.

176pp £1.50 Paperback ISBN 0 86130 016 5

THE COMMITTED MEN
(193mm x 125mm)

M John Harrison explores, in all its pain and horror, the world that is left to us after the Bomb has fallen and radiation spreads like cancer to drown those who survived the initial impact.

192pp £1.50 Paperback ISBN 0 86130 036 X

BY GAS MASK AND FIRE HYDRANT
(193mm x 125mm)

A revolutionary fantasy novel. Pre-Raphaelite Sword & Sorcery. If Aubrey Beardsley and Oscar Wilde were writing and illustrating today, the result would closely resemble this book. A guaranteed classic.

176pp £1.50 Paperback ISBN 0 86130 013 0

IN VIRICONIUM
(Collected in the Savoy anthology *New Wave Sword & Sorcery*)

A complete new Sword & Sorcery novelette set in the same milieu as *A Storm of Wings*.

SUSQUEMADELION
(Collected in the Savoy anthology *New Wave Sword & Sorcery*)

New visions of the Dwarf of All the World. "Susquemadelion lies in wait round the corner of your brain".

THE INCALLING
(Collected in the Savoy anthology *The Savoy Book*)

A metaphysical thriller in the best tradition of Charles Williams, but set in the London of the Seventies. A powerful modern story of spiritual exorcism.

"Ishmael Reed is probably the best black writer in America today"
The Village Voice

"Ishmael Reed must be, hands down, the most original poet/novelist working in the American language" – *San Fransisco Chronicle*.

MUMBO JUMBO
(193mm x 125mm)

In this HooDoo detective novel, private eyes PaPa LaBas and Black Herman investigate questions which have long plagued Mankind and New Yorkers too. Part vision, part satire, part farce, *Mumbo Jumbo* is a wholly original, unholy cross between the craft of fiction and witchcraft. A HooDoo thriller and an all-out assault on Western Civilisation. Illustrated.

240pp £1.50 Paperback ISBN 0 86130 042 4

THE LAST DAYS OF LOUISIANA RED
(193mm x 125mm)

Now Ed, founder of the Solid Gumbo empire, was dead – mysteriously, savagely, and eternally. It was clearly a case for PaPa LaBas, private eye and noonday HooDoo.

192pp £1.50 Paperback ISBN 0 86130 057 2

FLIGHT TO CANADA
(193mm x 125mm)

The rock'n'roll version of history. Raven Quickskill, not satisfied with leaving slavery halfway, has vowed to go the whole distance t Canada, a word that inspires as much fear throughout the South as 'revolt'.

192pp £1.50 Paperback ISBN 0 86130 056 4

THE FREE-LANCE PALLBEARERS
(913mm x 125mm)

Follow Bukka Doopeyduk into the futuristic never-never land of HARRY SAM, ex-used car salesman and Jehovah of the John. Bukka's odyssey for the true-believing Nazarene is at once surreal and chillingly familiar.

128pp £1.50 Paperback ISBN 0 86130 058 0

Mike Harding

Up the Boo Aye, Shooting Pookakies
(228mm x 152mm)

From the original Rochdale Cowboy, comedy star of tv and records, here is the ideal gift book for children and adults of all ages.

Inside this book you will meet strange creatures like the Grebs, the Diploblast, the Min and Fingummy the boot monster.

Don't let them frighten you for they are simply parts of your nightmares and nightmares as we know end when you wake up . . . or do they?

Up the Boo Aye, Shooting Pookakies is attractively designed with marvellous black and white artwork on every page and twelve sumptuous colour plates by splendid new artist Roger McPhail.

£2.50 Paperback ISBN 0 86130 059 9

The Thief of the World

By the same successful team, Mike Harding and Rodger McPhail. *The Thief of the World* is a scintillating collection of comic, curious and haunting tales based on the dance melodies of Ireland. Each tale is beautifully illustrated in full colour and has an accompanying music score for those adventurous enough to render the melodies themselves. These enchanting stories of legend, with their roots set firmly in the bogs and limestone crags of the West, make an enchanting book that will thrill and entertain all the family.

ISBN 0 86130 061 0   Details to be announced

RETURN FROM THE WILD
(193mm x 125mm)

The true story of Lassie, the red collie born wild in a
fox earth who, although devoted to her astonishing
owner, John Warren, remained to the outside world
very much a wild creature during her very full 16
years life span. Much has been said both for and
against the possibilities of Lassie being a hybrid Dog/
Fox. Genetics prove it to be impossible but the facts
in this book remain unanswerable. A beautifully
written and designed book for country and dog
lovers everywhere, with full colour plates by
naturalist painter Philip Snow and Derek Twiss. Also
contained are many photographs of Lassie, her owner
and her equally remarkable offspring.

192pp & 6 colour plates
£1.95 Paperback
ISBN 0 86130 062 9

SavoyBooks

279 Deansgate, Manchester M3 4EW, England.
Tel: 061-832 2168
IN ASSOCIATION WITH
NEW ENGLISH LIBRARY LTD.

JACK ON THE BOX
(193mm x 125mm)

The first book to collect Savoy's launch of Jack Trevor Story titles!

Fully illustrated with photographs from the television series *Jack on the Box* tells the story of the much publicised saga of Jack Trevor Story and Maggie. "As a passionate and often very funny account of a love affair (the saga) is a tour-de-force" – A.M. magazine.

160pp plus 4pp art insert £1.25 Paperback
ISBN 0 86130 025 4

THE MONEY GOES ROUND AND ROUND
(193mm x 125mm)

A whacky English farce about a writer who is rich and celebrated in Spain, but poor and ignored in England. Read how he tries to smuggle back a fortune in pesetas!

160pp £1.50 Paperback ISBN 0 86130 054 8

THE WIND IN THE SNOTTYGOBBLE TREE
(193mm x 125mm)

Spies, travel agents and all the ingredients of a Jack Trevor Story socio-mystery comedy.

172pp £1.50 Paperback ISBN 0 86130 055 6

Man Pinches Bottom
(193mm x 125mm)

Percy Paynter, professional comic strip writer and bird fancier by inclination goes to work in a lift and gets caught up in a case of mistaken identity in a murder hunt. "Our most talented living English comic novelist" – Michael Moorcock.

184pp £1.25 Paperback ISBN 0 86130 027 0

The Trouble with Harry
The classic novel filmed by Alfred Hitchcock
(193mm x 125mm)

Harry is a menace from the moment he turns up on the heath. For one long, hot maddening day he invades the lives of the inhabitants of the Sparrowswick Bungalow Estate, terrifying young Abie, puzzling the Captain, menacing Miss Gravely the spinster . . . No one knows what to do with him. The trouble with Harry is he's an embarrassment. The trouble with Harry is he's dead!

112pp £1.25 Paperback
ISBN 0 86130 035 1

The Screwrape Lettuce
(193mm x 125mm)

The Screwrape Lettuce is ". . . ironic . . . whimsical . . . volatile, grotesque, brilliantly messy – like watching a diamond burst in the hand. An appalling aphrodisiac is destroying the English, secret sex-police are taking over the country, and no one has yet noticed" – The Sunday Times. Illustrated by Robert Holland.

192pp £1.50 Paperback ISBN 0 86130 038 6

Savoy Books

279 Deansgate, Manchester M3 4EW, England.
Tel: 061-832 2168
IN ASSOCIATION WITH NEW ENGLISH LIBRARY LTD.

John Warren

Mike Harding

Ishmael Reed

Ken Reid

Gerald Scarfe

Langdon Jones

Charles Platt

M. John Harrison

Ken Reid

Published by Savoy Books in association with New English Library Ltd

Six large-size pictorial books

Now reprinted after more than thirty years, a set of major children's classics by one of Britain's great fantasy artists. The stories of Fudge the Elf show a quality rare in story-telling ability, and reveal a world of imagination and enchantment as believable and consistent as Professor Tolkein's "Lord of the Rings". Each book contains a set of superb colour plates.

FUDGE AND THE DRAGON
(335mm x 244mm)

First to be released, this tells of the exciting adventure of Fudge and Speck when they journey to the Land of Nowhere in search of a dragon's tooth, required to save their friend Blink, a woodland elf, from the effects of sorcery. An enthralling tale ideal as a gift for Christmas which will delight young and old alike.

128pp £3.50   ISBN 0 86130 007 6.

FUDGE IN BUBBLEVILLE
(335mm x 244mm)

Magic is once more the order of the day when a large, mud-eating monster appears in a lake near Fudge's home town of Pixieville, threatening all about with its terrifying presence. Fudge's most exciting adventure so far leads him to the underwater land of Bubbleville, and straight into the clutches of Golliponda, the wicked water witch, whose spitefulness to the sprites who live in Bubbleville is the cause of the trouble.

128pp £3.50   ISBN 0 86130 010 6.

FUDGE'S TRIP TO THE MOON
(335mm x 244mm)

FUDGE'S TRIP TO THE MOON tells of the perilous journey the little elf encounters when Speck's home-made rocket accidentally lifts-off — with Fudge inside! Fortunately the moon folk prove to be friendly, but not until more hazards and strange lunar lands have been braved.

128pp £3.50   ISBN 0 86130 011 4.

FUDGE IN TOFFEE TOWN
(335mm x 244mm)

The two elves are whisked off to the sugary planet of Plum-Duff in the invention of an extraordinary new visitor to Pixieville, Professor Nutt. On their arrival they are greeted by forests of cakes, mountains of blanc mange, seas of lemonade, people made of marzipan, as well as many unexpected perils and adventures in the land of Tummy-Ache!

128pp £3.50   ISBN 0 86130 008 4.

FUDGE TURNS DETECTIVE
(335mm x 244mm)

A series of mysterious robberies are solved when Fudge plays the role of detective. With the help of his friends Speck the Wood Elf, Bertie Bunn — to say nothing of Iu-Khan, the Egyptian Mummy and Woozle the Wizard — the thief is finally captured and his identity revealed.

128pp £3.50   ISBN 0 86130 009 2.

FROLICS WITH FUDGE
(335mm x 244mm)

Mistakenly offering help to a witch, Fudge and Speck are "rewarded" with a pair of magic gloves! But the gloves come alive and their invisible owner announces himself as King Bong, ruler of the kingdom of Downunder. The wicked witch has exiled the king from his people. But Fudge and Speck travel to the underground land and succeed in breaking the spell.

128pp £3.50   ISBN 0 86130 012 2

Gerald Scarfe

THE BOOK OF GERALD SCARFE
(345mm x 250mm)

This is Gerald Scarfe's first book in fourteen years.
For almost two decades Gerald Scarfe has established
his reputation as *the* social satirist of our time. His
work appears in most major magazines and newspapers
in England and America.

He is currently the resident cartoonist on the London
Sunday Times, and his most recent project, *The Wall*
is a film which features his animations and Pink
Floyd's music.

The Book of Gerald Scarfe consolidates his unique
vision with a varied selection of published work and
new drawings previewed in this collection for the first
time. The subjects include political caricatures and
savage portraits of contemporary icons, symbolic
drawings on themes such as religion, cruelty, sex,
power and greed – in general the whole spectrum of
social corruption.

"Certainly I can think of no other draughtsman in
Britain who, since the war, has shown more promise
in this genre" – *John Berger*

160pp £5.50 Paperback ISBN 0 86130 024 6
160pp £9.50 Hardcase ISBN 0 86130 028 9

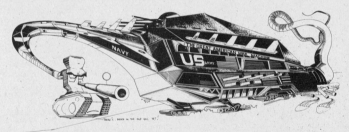

SavoyBooks

279 Deansgate, Manchester M3 4EW, England.
Tel: 061-832 2168
IN ASSOCIATION WITH NEW ENGLISH LIBRARY LTD.
TRADE COUNTER:
New English Library Ltd., Barnard's Inn, Holborn, London EC1N 2JR
Tel: 01-242 0767 Cables: NELPUBLISH LONDON; Telex: 21924

Savoy Rock'n'Roll

KISS
Robert Duncan
(193mm x 125mm)

America's premier rock'n'roll band tell their story in their own words. Kiss are the undisputed superstars of American stage-rock, and this best-selling book (half a million copies sold Stateside) introduces to English readers the Ninth Wonder of the Rock World. Fully illustrated with photographs of the band.

208pp £1.25 Paperback ISBN 0 86130 040 8

I AM STILL THE GREATEST SAYS JOHNNY ANGELO
Nik Cohn
(193mm x 125mm)

In a cool and highly original style Nik Cohn has written a bizarre fable of our time. Johnny Angelo is acknowledged as the definitive rock'n'roll novel. The book captures rock music's sickness and horror while staying true to its grandeur and allure.

176pp £1.25 Paperback ISBN 0 86130 041 6

(Also available the companion volume *Johnny Angelo says I am Still the Greatest*. 160pp £1.25 Paperback ISBN 0 86130 060 2)

JAMES DEAN: THE MUTANT KING
David Dalton
(193mm x 125mm)

"*The Mutant King* is a sensitive, haunting, psychological study . . . and David Dalton, in this fine, muscular book, has found the perfect words to preserve Dean's contribution to the 50s for posterity. An immensely important work, highly recommended" — Rex Reed. Fully illustrated.

400pp £1.95 Paperback ISBN 0 86130 043 2

THE ILLUSTRATED JAMES DEAN
(193mm x 125mm)

This fully illustrated overview of James Dean is comprised of some of the most sought after magazines devoted to the original teen rebel, and shows the dramatic impact Dean had on 1950's American culture. It makes available for the first time in twenty-five years a mass of neglected photographic material and, as well, provides a unique insight into the actor's life, both real and imaginary.

160pp £1.75 Paperback ISBN 0 86130 047 5

BLONDIE
Harry Doherty
(290mm x 210mm)

The first in the series of Savoy's large format colour illustrated rock'n'roll books. *Blondie* is packed with photographs of Debbie Harry, Chris Stein and band. Words by Melody Maker's rock critic Harry Doherty.

160pp £5.95 Paperback ISBN 0 86130 046 7

Forthcoming in the same series:
Led Zeppelin and *David Bowie*

SAVOY BOOKS LTD
279 Deansgate, Manchester M3 4EW, England. Tel: 061-832 2168
IN ASSOCIATION WITH NEW ENGLISH LIBRARY LTD.

TRADE COUNTER: New English Library Ltd., Barnard's Inn, Holborn, London EC1N 2JR Tel: 01-242 0767 Cables: NELPUBLISH LONDON; Telex: 21924